T0344069

THE WELL

The Quest for a Global Cure is…

THE WELL

"A Fountain for Life; or A Pool of Death"

By
R. Chapman Wesley

Registered WGAw

@2023; 1-8876313911

R. Chapman Wesley

info@hightoppublishing.com

"I will give unto him that is a thirst
of the fountain of the water of Life freely"

REVELATIONS 21:6

"First, do no harm."

HIPPOCRATES
460–370 B.C.

"The town may change. But *The Well* cannot be changed.
All draw from *The Well*.
But if the rope is short, or the jug breaks,
MISFORTUNE!"

KING WEN
Channeling Lao Tzu

FOREWORD

In "The Well," physician and writer, R. Chapman Wesley, has penned a mythical story, paralleling the cataclysmic issues of our time.

What if a singular scientific discovery could substantiate an ancient legend and "fulfill the quest for perfect health, and the yearning for a disease-free life of extra-normal vitality during a lifespan of one's own choosing?"

But what if that same discovery, in corrupt and evil hands, might lead to the malevolent extortion of power and wealth and world domination through the threat of certain death?

This is the dilemma that physician-scientist, Dr. Rex Lee, must confront in an epic journey of synchronous events in which he departs the modern world of scientific discovery and arrives to a fateful rendezvous with "The Unseen."

Secluded from our world, "The Unseen" are an indigenous tribe, who are the Keepers of the Secrets and the Protectors of "The Well." It is they who have discovered that the true "Well" lies within each of us, already an embedded perfection of ourselves, given by the One Universal Mind, simply awaiting a recognition to unleash the perfection.

Although our understanding of reality and our wonderous use of its knowledge can be increasingly described by a multiplicity of mathematical concepts, equations, and numbers, "The Unseen" understand, resonate with, apply, and manifest the simple concept that "One is the Only Number, and that the Only Number is One." From this standpoint, resonance with The One is a basis by which an individual mind can foster any new creation, any new reality, including the gift of perfect health.

In his modern Odyssey, R. Chapman Wesley has made an excellent case for drawing sustenance from "The Well" and has delivered a fast-paced, mystery-driven, visual, cinematic epic.

—James Redfield,
Author of *The Celestine Prophecy*

INTRODUCTION

According to Lao Tzu, The Well, an image of nature combining the qualities of water and wood, is an inexhaustible source of nourishment to all. From this mystical source, always available, success in any aspect of one's life is dependent upon withdrawing a sufficient amount. We can take as much as we desire, for it is freely given. A necessary step is simply the recognition that it is always there, always available.

The outpourings that have filled My Well arise from many sources, some known and some very unknown. Childhood exposures to oceans, lakes, and rivers have played definite roles.

From college days to this day, The I Ching commentary, propagated by seemingly random probability, but somehow based on a subconscious synchronicity, has informed the intuitive side of my life. Randomly juxtaposing states of nature, The I Ching reveals 64 conditions defining the relationship of individuals to each other, to nature, to society/government, to the Divine, and the Divine to everything. My inquiry has been amplified by the poetry of the Tao Te Ching and the concept of an inscrutable Tao, or The Way, from which everything emerges.

Fascination with numbers has had a profound effect upon me. Numbers seem to govern the entire universe. The patterns in numbers, like the Fibonacci Sequence, are deducible from ever-accumulating observations and provide ever-increasing insight and clarity to our approximations of the universe and reality itself.

We may never truly know what; but we can increasingly know how.

The study of clinical hypnosis has also been profoundly important. I cannot do justice to this subject except to say that hypnosis is one of the most important and cost-effective tools in clinical medicine that is currently not being widely applied.

I would be truly remiss not to mention the writings of Ernest Holmes and his seminal work, "The Science of Mind," which I have endeavored to study daily in some form for several decades and to James Redfield's The Celestine Prophecy, an overpowering influence.

I have always been fascinated by art in general and the study of African Art promulgated by Prof. Robert F. Thompson's African Art 78B, my favorite Yale undergraduate course.

I love the deeply spiritual, modern works and paintings of Abdul Mati Klarwein and hope that you might seek them out.

During residency, I had exposure to immunology, virology, infectious diseases, and oncology, none of which underpin my career scope of practice (cardiology).

My lifelong concern over global health threats, originally regarding the threat of nuclear weapons, propelled me toward pandemic inquiry and preparation since the initial bird flu scares of 2003.

Having said all that, the imaginings of this book should not be viewed as science. I totally made the whole thing up, well in advance of the Coronavirus Pandemic. My initial inklings came in Thailand in the spring of 2018, followed by a story outline composed in Shanghai Airport on my return flight to the U.S. That led to the first draft of a screenplay in summer 2018. After many drafts, the story congealed into a novel and an audio book.

Hopefully you find "*The Well*" entertaining and lending some measure of insight into the human condition. That is all an artist, and hopefully any scientist, can hope for.

THE WELL

CHAPTER 1

THE MONK

It was Quantum Cold. Well below absolute zero. From a complete absence of vibration, it emerged, phantoms of energy, randomly flipping into and out of existence. Wavelets collided and coalesced into particles of matter and then congealed into molecules of oxygen, bound to hydrogen of varying density. It was water, the basis of Life Itself. It was *The Well*.

Across the heavens, it was to this most subtle of all vibrations that the Monk awoke.

In Truth, it was a vibration no more random than any pathway sustaining Life, compelled into existence by unseen laws of nature, by the Design of a Single Universal Mind, Whose Thought would now impel the thinking to choose, to grow, and to evolve... to grasp the Perfection underlying All Things.

Just as in countless times before, *The Well* became the Sperm, swimming upon gravitational waves, again falling toward an uncertain outcome, but unlike before, now an outcome based upon mankind's choice. Not just gravity. It was Attraction. And as before, The Earth was its Egg.

While seated on red curtains of satin, the Monk's eyes opened upon a golden pot. It had been foretold by the vicar, eons ago...

He, the Monk, now Buddhist and a disciple of Lao Tzu, would be a link in the chain of destiny.

As instructed, he picked up the yarrow sticks and threw them. And there it was…the image, juxtaposing two states of Nature:

Outward Fire, expanding up and burning Wood, projecting the inner Wind of an invisible force, penetrating all elements of Heaven and Earth, the image of a golden nutrient pot, roasting on a spiritual fire, the symbol by which collective awareness might manifest in a single man or a single woman. The Cauldron, the receptacle for the waters of *The Well*.

But who were to be The Invisible People?

In the chain of causation, it was not his to choose or determine. His was to subsume the vision, and, in its recognition, set in motion the journey.

Having confirmed the image, he closed his eyes, and once again, the vision sprang forth.

The Well, a vibrant crystal, blossomed out of nothingness. It aggregated rock and ice and tumbled toward warming sunlight. A luminous trail of agitated ions released a vibratory force that echoed through the vacuum of cold, dark space and focused upon an emerging Earth, blue of ocean and green of land.

The spot to which it would arrive had already been determined by Mind, gravity, and the struggles of mindful men long gone. It was simply the task of the Monk to observe.

Screaming through the ionosphere, the tumbling rock convulsed in a suffocating air blast. A fiery crystal cone of green, it shredded the vacant air before it, through the dusk of day, magnifying and illuminating rolling vistas of verdant rainforest that oscillated over hills and valleys of river tributaries.

The mating calls of tropical fowl fell silent.

Slanting across a gushing mountainous waterfall feeding the river below, the meteor crashed into a river-fed pond, buckling but not breaking the palms surrounding it, ejecting water into a vibrant funnel mist. The crystalline meteorite glowed in a cratered center, hesitated, then downward burrowed, sucking the remaining water into a swirling green whirlpool.

From a geocentric orbit, over a land mass he could hardly imagine much less observe, the Monk saw a pinpoint flash of light in his mind's eye that became indelibly seared into his consciousness.

Now, far too old himself, it would be to this place he would charge his Chinese adept, Ch'ien, the Modest, to initiate the Cauldron's journey. How or when it would get there was uncertain. His years of dedicated study and his own experience had taught him that the path to mankind's enlightenment was a circuitous one, promised by Mind but dependent on struggle. Only through the enlightenment of the self-chosen few could the base instincts of the selfish to subjugate the world, be overthrown.

The Monk deeply pondered this last thought as he exited his snow drown temple into the still, but frigid Himalayan air.

Why had his thought migrated into emotion?

Now, nearing the end of his life, he so much wished that the promise of *The Well* could be realized. The promise of Mind's awareness that he, though learned, was only beginning to accept beyond the taint of his solitary perspective. Could it finally be universally experienced?… The power of feeling, recognizing, and revealing one's own perfection, the power of any man or woman to empower his or her own destiny, his or her own identity, the Power of *The Well*?

One deep, whole inhalation. Suddenly, without exhaling, a shattering contortion squeezed his gut and forced him to his knees. He could not visualize the future, but the cataclysms of past impacts rushed forth. With each mass death, new life had sprung forth. Could Mind intend or even allow mankind's march toward enlightenment to die? But having given man choice, was it even Mind's Choice to make? The riddle he had never considered had shaken him to his core.

Back into the temple he returned to frame the warning. Throughout the night, he arranged the ancient Chinese characters:

"Jing"

"*The Well*: A Fountain for Life; or A Pool of Death."

CHAPTER 2

CHIEN THE MODEST

The night was very young. But he was not. Or so he wished to seem.

A tattered, Yak-clothed, white-haired, elderly Chinese traveler, carrying a large bamboo cane, shuffled through the light snow of a vacant village. The cane did not seem to aid him. He held it out in front of him with two clenched fists, skimming the snow, as if rowing,

There were none present other than him to hear. Now perfectly motionless, the rumbling of the ground below, felt through his Yak-pelt boots, signaled the approach of a marauding horde of thieves with no honor among them. These men were undisciplined barbarians, barely controllable. They required the constant supervision of a tyrannical warlord.

His master, the Monk, had warned him of such a moment. His master had expressed the concern that he, Chien the Modest, although a long-studied adept, may have over-planned the moment. Chien had not exhibited the traits of spontaneous adaptability and creativity that the Monk felt Chien would need to complete his share of the mission.

To compensate, Chien strove to plan for every contingency, endeavoring always to do his best, yet being consciously aware of being consciously non-intuitive.

It seemed necessary. The warlord had many spies. His greed for the golden pot was only matched by the depth of his treachery.

The rumor of the warlord's coming had vacated the village but perhaps had not constrained a bevy of traitorous observers, whose information was paramount despite their apparent absence.

Chien rushed to one of the spots he had previously designated. In a trench covered with brush at the village's edge, he observed the warlord at the head of his calvary, driving forward into the middle of the town. The warlord halted his horse and looked around.

Summoning over three captains, the warlord barked out orders. The captains then rallied their horsemen into three squads. The warlord with the first part galloped ahead through the narrow village street. The remaining groups turned right and left, weaving themselves into trees surrounding the village.

Then toward the direction from which the horde had come, Chien ran, obscured by roadside trees.

Now, his plan would be set. To succeed, he would have to go through one part of the calvary, avoid another, and arrive at the monastery before the third.

But then what? What about the escape?

He reflected.

According to the master, Life often finds a way to illuminate a different path.

• • •

Down the side of a rocky hill, Chien galloped upon his trusty steed; then through a cavern to claim the stash he'd need.

He arrived at the mouth of a mountain cave obscured by heavy brush. Dismounting, he pulled aside snow-tinged leaves to reveal rows of liquid filled gourds, attached together by woven ropes.

· · ·

Through the valley below, Chien led his horse on foot with four of the gourds slung over the animal's back. With a flickering oil lamp in hand, he weaved through a growth of trees.

Upon reaching a flat, grassy plain, Chien strained his eyes to see the outline of a structure at the far edge, barely visible from the trees surrounding it.

After traversing the plain, he could clearly see a five-sided, one-story wooden pyramid sitting on a pentagonal base with a golden eye emblazoned in the middle of each triangular side. The structure had no entrance. At the back side, Chien scuffed snow aside, revealing a trap door.

Chien went through the trap door with the oil lamp in hand and emerged inside the small structure. There before him was a one-horse sled. Inside the sled was a small black glass jar.

Walking behind the sled, Chien found a wooden crank attached to the wall. He turned the handle clockwise. The opposite wall lifted outward and upward, opening the pyramid. Chien removed the gourds from his horse, securing them inside the sled. He attached the harness of the sled to the horse, tied his trusty bamboo cane to the saddle, and drove the sled out.

Later, after placing a clump of snow into the small black glass jar, shaking it, and returning it to the pocket of his coat, Chien turned around to appreciate the spectacle.

Torrents of upward spiraling, tornado-like flames engulfed the wooden pyramid.

• • •

From his perch in the monastery's highest tower, the Monk saw Chien's fiery eruption in the distant valley below. Perhaps the fire, if seen, would provide a diversion, giving him time by deflecting opposition away from an inevitable rendezvous. But he could not count on that. Now, there was no time to lose.

The Monk rapidly descended dark, narrow, winding tower steps and entered a voluminous but bare vestibule, devoid of richly appointed golden ornaments, statues, and relics.

In the lotus position, the Monk sat on red satin covering a cold stone slab. He reached down before him, gathered the pot, now covered in black paint, wrapped it in a white cloth, and placed it into a satchel. Rolling up a globe -like map into a scroll covered with Chinese characters, he placed it along with an eagle feather stylet into a tube, then sealed it tightly.

Lastly, he reached behind, grabbed a sheathed short sword, and placed it in front of his crossed knees.

• • •

The soft slushing of his one-horse sled was finally interrupted. Behind him, Chien could hear the approaching commotion of pounding hooves just around the bend. Chien pulled out the black glass jar from his fleeced coat pocket and gulped down its contents. He then opened a gourd and took a swig. Then Chien, like a drunken sage, began to hum as loudly as he could.

The pounding of hooves grew louder and faster. Horsemen approached him from behind with swords drawn. The captain of the troop rode up to and alongside Chien's sled. He looked into the eyes of an inebriated sage. He smiled and then sheathed his sword. The surrounding horsemen laughed.

And just where was the sage going, the captain asked. The sage replied that he was going home with as little of his drink as possible. Several horsemen offered to help the sage with that.

The sage held out the gourd toward the captain. The captain shook his head. His horsemen chided him. Relenting, he took a swig. A particularly emboldened soldier rode up and took the gourd from him. The man took a mighty gulp and passed it to the other riders.

When the near empty gourd was passed back to the sage, he slurped the remaining contents and then threw it, as if a grenade, to the ground. The horsemen laughed. The captain announced that they would officially escort the old sage as they were going in the same direction. Chien nodded.

Standing by his horse, Chien reached behind him and surreptitiously detached the harness of the sled. He then slung around his bamboo cane and poked the captain off his horse.

As the captain thudded to the ground, Chien galloped away with abandon. Shocked and confused troops waited for the captain to rise. The captain screamed at his men and jumped on his horse. The militia frantically gave chase with bows and arrows drawn.

At first spears, and then arrows whisked by Chien's ears. But as Chien galloped onward, veering right and then left, the volume of murderous projectiles fell off precipitously as men, suddenly overwhelmed by tunnel vision, fell from their horses.

Finally, alone with no charges behind him, and with no need for further concealment, Chien stopped, removed a white wig from his head, smudged makeup from his cheeks, and projected the boyish, smiling face of a 16-year-old.

From a hilltop below the tree line, Chien looked up to the darkened mountain monastery. A solitary lamp waved from a high window. Chien galloped toward the monastery.

● ● ●

The warlord stood sternly, facing his cavalry. With captains in front, three groups awaited in rows to the left, the right and the middle. The warlord gestured to each captain to come forward. They stopped and each bowed with respect. But as they rose, the warlord whipped out his sword and beheaded all three delinquent captains. The warlord raised his bloody sword over his head. Concealing their fear, the horsemen yelled in boisterous approval.

The warlord mounted his horse. The horde followed. Together they galloped out of the clearing on a rendezvous with the monastery. The warlord was now convinced that the golden pot had never been moved from there.

● ● ●

The elation Chien had recently experienced had waned. Feelings of dread, once imagined, suddenly became real. This might be the very last time that he would ever see his master.

Chien moved through a long vacant hallway toward a solitary torch in the vestibule. Once he passed through the entrance, buttressed by massive twin stone doors, he saw the Monk sitting on red satin with his implements before him.

Standing before the Monk, Chien blinked in a vain attempt to suppress the tears welling up in his eyes. The attempt failed. A tear rolled down his cheek.

The Monk gestured to Chien to sit. But embarrassed by his emotions, Chien preferred to stand. Chien attempted to speak. But he could only mumble an incoherent utterance between unmoving lips. The Monk smiled and raised his index finger.

Reaching up, the Monk handed the satchel to Chien and gestured that Chien should look inside. Chien nodded after he saw the pot and the sealed tube.

Chien then focused on the short sword in front of the Monk's crossed knees and frowned. The Monk nodded, picked up the sword, smiled, and held it out toward Chien.

At first a rattling, then the clamoring of heavily armed men echoed increasingly louder through the vast hallway.

The Monk pointed to a cabinet far behind him.

And then the Monk whispered his final instructions.

"Now go. Complete the mission. Do not turn back."

Chien scurried to the louvered cabinet. He entered and looked back through the slats. His master sat calmly, surely awaiting his end.

Chien opened the back of the cabinet. There were steps that led down to a cave, pre-lit with torches placed at 50-yard intervals. Chien ran down the steps. The time seemed like an eternity compiled upon the complexity of emotions he felt. But it was actually a very short moment before Chien had stopped, turned and retraced his steps. Despite no hope of succeeding, how could he leave his master behind?

Through the louvers, Chien observed the warlord towering over his master, still as placid as Chien had left him. The warlord grunted loudly and shook with agitated gesticulations. The Monk sat immobile. Chien hoped beyond reason that the Monk had transformed himself into an impenetrable stoned statue, impervious to defacement, harm, and certain death.

Suddenly hope vanished. The moment had finally come.

The warlord unsheathed his sword, raised it with both arms above his shoulders, closed his eyes, and swung downward at the Monk's neck. When the blade slashed through vacant air, the startled hands of the warlord, meeting no resistance, relinquished the sword. The sword flew spinning backwards. A trapdoor within the stone slab had sprung open. The Monk then submerged below the floor just before the stone slab slammed tight.

As if he himself was beheaded, Chien's head slammed upward and thudded against the wooden cabinet, startling the warlord and his men. Chien rapidly scurried back down the steps, descending through the cave. He unsheathed the short sword, sliced off the heads of each torch, and then stepped upon them extinguishing each flame, as he ran by.

Chien could hear the angry shouts of vengeful men in darkness several hundred yards behind him.

Chien came to a deep hole in the center of the cave that he had previously encountered. As before, he navigated around a bifurcating ledge. After carefully traversing around the hole, Chien took the overhanging torch and tossed it into the deep cavern. After many seconds, the descending torch finally splashed into a subterranean creek.

Continuing to run, Chien stopped momentarily as he heard the screams of terrified soldiers falling through the crevasse.

• • •

Down the side of the mountain, Chien rode on his trusted steed along a creek that merged with other creeks into a rapid flowing river.

The hope that he had eluded his pursuers vanished.

While one group of the horsemen had fallen through the mountain cave's abyss, the other groups were with the warlord, awaiting his appearance below the monastery. Now they were in hot pursuit merely a quarter of a mile behind him.

As Chien approached a more level plateau, the river widened out, and the flow over deposits of rocks slowed down before the river narrowed again at the precipice of a steep waterfall.

At the side of the slow flowing river, with the satchel and his bamboo cane in hand, Chien jumped off his horse and gave him a tearful hug. He then slapped his rump. Without hesitation the horse galloped ahead and jumped over the waterfall.

To Chien's amazement, the horse landed upright and then

gently swam downstream. Chien was both happy and despondent. Why had he not ridden the horse? Surely, he would not survive the fall by himself. There was only one option now.

Chien ran to the edge of the river surrounded by high grass and reeds. He submerged himself below the surface and breathed air through the hollow bamboo cane.

The warlord and his men rode up to the side of the river. Looking over the precipice of the waterfall, in the distance, the warlord could see the outline of the swimming horse with no rider, floating effortlessly downstream.

Unconvinced, the warlord instructed his men to walk around and line the perimeter of the river. Chien could hear them approaching. He was certain that he would be seen.

With one hand on the cane, Chien reached with the other hand into the satchel and pulled out the short sword and the pot. He exhaled through the cane and then took in the largest possible gulp of air. Pulling the cane down, he severed off a two-foot section, and tossed the remainder away under water.

Inverting the pot above his head, Chien raised his body upward by pushing his feet on the rocks of the vertical shoreline. Finally with all his might, he pushed the pot above the water and then pulled the air-filled pot down. After submerging as deep as he could, he inhaled the air in the pot through the shortened bamboo cane and then exhaled along the side of the pot.

Finally, the warlord in his men grew tired of waiting. They mounted their horses and rode away.

Chien emerged from the river with the pot, the tube in the satchel, and the diminutive bamboo cane. He collapsed in exhaustion on the shore.

In a snow-covered shack, high on the mountain above the monastery, the Monk in deep meditation, opened his eyes and smiled.

THE SEEN WORLD

CHAPTER 3

POPOV

The sheer beauty of cresting, frothing, and bending waves offered Anatoly Mikhailovich Popov momentary respite from the momentous work that consumed him. He allowed himself only briefly to be seduced by bright sun, peerless white clouds, reflected white sand, and the ensemble of curvaceous and multicolored women that meandered Ipanema Beach.

He was a true swashbuckler of a man, still vigorous deep in his seventies, somewhat darker than the average Russian. For the purpose of disguise, lightening of his skin would have been a better choice. The contrast of olive skin against overflowing dyed-white hair, beard, and moustache and his wire-rim, oval glasses made him stand out as a mulatto Leon Trotsky.

How reckless of him! It was now late at night as he peered across the boite (a night club) to the rotating bottom of a statuesque dark-haired young woman, that seemed to beckon him at every turn.

Would such diversions become his downfall? Perhaps. Yet he was convinced that he had foiled the dragnets of multiple intelligence services. Besides, the night-time girls of the night-time clubs loved him, back then and even now. After this was over, how delightful it would be to be entwined in not just one but all of them, the further pursuit of the young life he started in Leningrad.

Could there be any more confirmation than the brightened smiling face of the fit and flexible young woman in front of him? Was she coming back for more? He thought not. She just liked the frisky old man.

Popov lowered his gaze, closed his eyes, and reflected upon the important work yet to be done.

As he exited the club, two redheads hugged him as Popov delivered to each a generous tip. Outside as he slowly walked away, Popoff tipped his hat to new girls as they arrived, each secretly hoping for a future chance to rumble with the generous old man. After all, the eldest attendants had long declared him to be the expert at the horizontal lambada.

• • •

When the elevator doors of the Copacabana resort hotel opened, it took a while for Popoff to move given his drowsiness. He shuffled down the hall, stopped in front of his hotel room, and uncharacteristically struggled to find his plastic access.

Inside his otherwise darkened hotel room, moonlight streamed through the double doors to a balcony overlooking the well-lit cove of Copacabana Beach. Popoff bathed his face in the moonlight with closed eyes and breathed in the balmy breeze. He tottered back toward the foot of his king-size bed and plopped into it, fast asleep.

• • •

Intense afternoon sunlight alone upon Popov's face was not enough to stir him. But one intense rumble of the bus finally chastened his wistfulness. Now fully awake, in the rear seat, he looked toward the left. Above high rises whisking by, he saw the expansive arms of Christ the Redeemer. But he was not ready yet to receive the invitation.

With a sigh, he opened his briefcase. He pushed aside hermetically sealed, biohazard labelled vials and a necklace. Removing a scroll, he pondered rows of Chinese characters.

• • •

Unbeknownst to Popov, minutes later and only miles away, the placid calm of stress-free Copacabana Beach gave way to a massive, unmarked van that invaded closed-off traffic lanes reserved for weekend runners, walkers, bikers, and lookers. With assistance of motorcycle cops, the van turned ocean-ward down a two lane, one-way street. Two blocks in, it backed into a hotel loading dock and jarred against the landing.

Inside, bilateral blue bulbs dimly lit the van. In the far recess, faint light shown upon four men so heavily encased in orange biohazard gear that their faces were totally obscured.

Next to them, in rows on each side, sat heavily armed SWAT troops in close-quarter-battle (CQB) gear. These troops were experienced, battle tested. In conflicts with drug traffickers during favela wars, they had endured house to house searches among IED infested traps, come under heavy automatic fire, dodged RPGs, and stormed prison riots. But none of them were ready for the new threat, just learned.

The images were still stark and vivid in their collective mind. The bioethicist's photos and videos revealed large pustular skin eruptions oozing from cavities of face, limb, and core; blood dripping from every orifice...from nose, mouth, ears, rectum, and vagina; and the vacant eyes of those that took too long to die. The pictures were of pigmented men, women, and children, nameless victims of a nameless village in a remote and nameless country.

Why should this have even been revealed to them? Some thought they were better off not knowing. What good was the signing of a pre-lecture authorization without the protective gear to bolster their duty?

How could the intelligence service have missed the threat? Rumors abounded that the terrorists or terrorist had operated freely in the country for some time, aided by clandestine corruption, in collusion with hostile foreign powers. Rio was no picnic, but it was certainly not a hotbed of competitive multinational intrigue, or so they had thought.

A sniper team on the roof of an adjacent hotel had a commanding view of the hotel entrance but had no understanding of the potential terror that might unfold. They had not been given any authorizations to sign. They were under the strict orders of a separate entity within the entity. They were charged to take down anyone with an infra-red locator signal, either attached or focused on the body.

A white stretch bullet proof limousine with six doors pulled up to a circular entrance. Three men in dark suits exited from the middle row and hovered under a spherical glass awning at the entrance. A bell man opened the passenger door. The man who controlled the signal, Tom Stern, hedge fund manager of Bio Acquisitions International (BAI), exited the limo and entered with two of the men. The third remained outside and chain smoked.

Inside a chandelier lobby, one man sat in an armchair and focused on the entrance; the other sat at the corner of the bar and scanned the elevator. Neither of these two men, employees of BAI, knew of Stern's true intent, sworn duty to the security of the United States.

Although not a scientist, Stern's detective work on all phases of the CDC's bioterrorism prevention regime had paid off. His consultations with carefully screened experts had borne fruit.

After having studied Popov intensely, Stern concluded that Popov would store the virus in an inert form. Although the role of radiation was unclear, the hallways of the hotel had been scanned for the very minutest traces of a particular signature. If found, finding the virus on premise would be certain. Keeping the subject alive at that point would be far less important.

Although public assassination might be quite messy in the conspiracy-ridden Brazilian press, the scandal of unauthorized research performed by Genometrics, but funded by the U.S. government, would remain suppressed. The first exposure mimicked the first cluster of spontaneous Ebola outside of Africa. The second had been the release of an altered virus onto a Bronx subway to track the rapidity of its spread. Neither was the work of Popov. In fact, Stern was clueless of Popov's aim and motives.

When the man outside stopped smoking and crushed out his cigarette, Stern walked to the reception desk and showed a head shot of Popov to a clerk. She was taken aback. Immediately, she entered an inner office and returned with the hotel manager.

The manager looked long and hard at the photo. "Desculpe, I am sorry, Señor. This man has not returned to his room."

CHAPTER 4

THE CAULDRON

The bus was finally ascending the serpentine cobblestone roads of hilly Santa Teresa. It had taken a detoured path after traffic had been abruptly diverted along the Botafogo Bay. Time was running out, and Popov had to focus, especially on the most recent celestial finding.

Perhaps, it was the vibrant colors of spectrographs defining the chemical compositions of galactic gas clouds that had distracted him. Now, he recollected a blur outside the bus window during a momentary stoppage in Copacabana near Leme. An apparition in his peripheral vision, a statuesque feline figure in a taut black spandex body suit, running southward along the beach toward some traffic-related commotion.

Could it have been her? Could she be the Vamp from Genometrics?

Could it have been Vitkin's Bitch?

Surely, Vitkin would have profiled any weakness. Could one night of license have done him in? Increasingly, he was realizing that his part of the journey was coming to an end.

Anxiety rose within him. Timing was everything. After all, the universe seemed to be imbued with an inexplicable synchronicity.

Would Doctor Lee be ready if it fell to him? Lately during his day hours, Popov tried to visualize him. But in the dream time, he had seen a woman.

Although fraught with urgency, he lapsed into reflection, an urge to put his own life into perspective.

It was at the feet of his grandfather, the forebear of anti-Bolshevik white Russians, who managed to bury their gold in eastern Siberia, that he first heard of the legend... the quest for perfect health, the yearning for a disease-free life of extra-normal vitality during a life span of one's own choosing.

There was none more smitten by the quest than Sergei Abrahamovich Popov, architect, scientist, archeologist, paleontologist, metaphysician to physicians, lyricist, and spinner of vivid yarns. And none more captivated by his pronouncements than his grandson Popov, then, of course, called Anatoly.

At the age of 7, Popov spent the entire summer with his Papai, as he called him, at the blue dacha under the blue sky of the Crimean shore, a welcome respite from brutal Siberian winters and restrictive parents. Here, Popov's imagination soared on wings of incredible universal myths; all of which he was convinced, had some basis in fact, including that of a Traveling Star bringing Heaven on Earth to mankind.

After that summer, he rejoined his family who had relocated near Vladivostok.

Living by water had become important for Popov. During summer months, he resided at the very tip of the Kamchatka Peninsula at a point where each day he could observe both sunrise and sunset, rising and setting in Asian waves.

To shield him from communist influence, Popov was ordered to an orthodox monastery by ultra-religious parents, where he was mentored, paradoxically by a learned monk, in all matters of science and math, secretly shunning all manner of doctrinal orthodoxy. Popov inculcated the monk's fascination with eastern mysticism. It was then, not surprising, that Popov would gravitate as a Soviet youth ambassador to southern China, before traveling west to finish his formal education.

It was near Canton while secretly studying Kung Fu in a Taoist temple that Popov first encountered the Legend of *The Well*... of an Unworldly Visitor, carrying the power of healing thought to a distant invisible tribe. They were the Ones who had received a golden Chinese pot, The Cauldron, by which the secret might be revealed to the world, but at a time and place of their choosing.

When he finally arrived at University in Leningrad, Popov found he had extraordinary aptitude in science and girls, both of which came extremely easy for him. Fascination with *The Well* drove him to biology, virology, and immunology; the government's quest for World Sovietization pushed him into bioterrorism.

While international bodies decried the use of such weapons, his overseers pushed hard for the creation of biological weapons "without fingerprints" as a counter measure to the threat of US nuclear weapons during the Vietnam War. In response, Popov both sped up and slowed down the Soviet effort.

A student of Buddhism, Popov was particularly unnerved by two images of the war; that of a Buddhist monk, Kwon Duc, who splashed upon his body gasoline, and burned himself alive on June 11, 1963 in protest of the Saigon government, and the assassination of a Viet Cong by General Nguyen Ngoc Loan during the Tet Offensive of 1968.

Although involved in bioweapons development during the 80's, Popov investigated ways to enhance the body's immunity using viral genes. It would later be proven an effective measure against some cancers. But then, Popov had an incredible leap of intuition. Perhaps an element in *The Well* could lead to total immunity.

In the 90's, during a visit to Belgrade, he defected to the West and worked primarily on counter measures to bioterrorism. Thereafter, Popov spent most of his discretionary time questing for *The Well* in China, studying Taoism and volunteering on archeological excavations under close Chinese supervision and surveillance until they concluded he was a "nut."

On an excavation of a temple built by Ch'ien the Modest, he found a 300-year-old copy of a scroll in Portuguese, of a 2000 year old Chinese map, alluding to *The Well*, pinpointing as if from space, to a discrete location in the Amazon of Brazil, not far from the border with Colombia.

The Portuguese were not only a maritime colonial power, but also incomparable map makers. After searching all of Macao, Popov lucked out when he approached a premier antique map dealer, Najib Hakim Rhakman. He was a man of Arab Malaysian descent, a venomous privateer in early life, who had found solace in the Koran.

From this dealer and purveyor of pirate legend, he heard the story of Portuguese slave traders who had discovered the golden pot, camouflaged in lead. It was secretly carried by a Taoist monk, disguised as one of them. They stole it from the monk and murdered him in Macao just prior to their passage across the Pacific. Their greed had them visualizing an endless cavern of gold, from which they believed the pot was derived.

The marauders sailed east with Filipino slaves, none of which survived the passage. In 1728, these Portuguese arrived in Spanish controlled Colombia at Buenaventura, under intense suspicion as slavers with no slaves, at the very onset of a colonial slave rebellion. They secretly transported the pot as none could agree upon a trustworthy location to hide it.

On the journey through central Colombia, they battled thieves and the elements. After passing Iquitos, cliques formed, and fought among themselves. When they reached the Amazonas, only a few had survived native attacks and malaria. The dealer's story ended there.

But years later in Manaus, Brazil, Popov heard a tale that one pirate, the only Englishman among them, had reached the tribe with the pot. There he miraculously recovered from a terminal parasitic illness. He repented, married into the tribe, and bore many children. When Popov asked for the name of the tribe, none knew. Moreover, none of the tribe had ever been encountered. While traveling along the Rio Solimo off the Amazon River, Popov was told that the tribesmen were miraculously invisible.

Popov felt an insistent tug on his left shoulder.

The bus had reached the pinnacle of its route on the top of Santa Teresa. All the remaining passengers had exited and waited across the street for a transfer.

Popov gathered everything into his briefcase. When he

descended the stairs, his dark glasses fell out of his pocket. The wheel of a passing bike crushed them. "C'est la vie," he thought, but he couldn't stop staring at the shattered lens.

With short heel-to-toe steps, he carefully traversed the steep, stony winding descent. It would not be far to the secret laboratory over the years he had meticulously assembled.

CHAPTER 5

THE AMULET

The ante room in the basement of the renovated colonial hillside mansion had the musty smell of a subterranean cavern. The odor would incite in Popov a sense of discovery whenever he would open the door to the cellar after long absences.

He shut the door behind him and in darkness pulled a hanging cord. A swinging bulb cast light and shadow as he walked with his briefcase and stepped in front of a stainless-steel door. Now the smell was particularly strong. There had been no need to return without the critical final data.

Mostly, Popov had to wait upon conceptual and technological advances in astrophysics and quantum analysis in order to define the characteristics of the crystal he was seeking. He used the time wisely, assembling each investigative innovation as needed, then later selling off the unnecessary equipment or technology.

Isolating, altering, and removing the potential viral bioweapon without notice had taken surprisingly little time and, with Popov's stature, was surprisingly easy. But the theft, once discovered, had triggered a world-wide dragnet by different forces, each concealing their search for different reasons.

He turned a wheel-like knob, entered, and sealed the massive door of the lab behind him. The lights turned on in sequence. The lab looked like a modest geological mineral exhibit except for a table mounted laser, targeted upon a vise-like receptacle for analysis.

Rows of stones and crystals housed in stacked glass drawers, were meticulously sorted and identified by the latitude and longitude of suspected Amazonian locations. Now with the astrophysical data, Popov had a very good idea of which crystal to look for. Tension in his entire upper torso ratcheted up.

He picked out a green crystal, placed it in a vise, activated the laser, and killed the lights. In darkness, a concentrated beam of light penetrated the crystal and splintered into a kaleidoscopic prism. The split screen images on his computer monitor matched.

Popov sighed in relief, but only momentarily. He sensed that the net was closing in. The chances were slim that he would ever reach the location and obtain the necessary critical mass of crystal.

He would now have to take the risk to stake the journey of his life on Dr. Lee. He would have to go to Plan B. And for that reason, just in case, he would need a Plan C. Popov sat down next to the computer, loaded a file, and ejected a thumb drive.

He removed the crystal from the vise, opened his briefcase, took out a necklace, and then inserted the crystal into a central amulet. He then searched the website of SETI (Search for Extraterrestrial Intelligence) and downloaded the page for Gia Marina Lee, PhD, in the Section of Astrobiology.

Popov then placed printed pages and the necklace into the briefcase next to biohazard-labelled tubes and closed the case.

• • •

Tubular fluorescent bulbs hanging from a dull gray ceiling, flickered, buzzed, and then projected continuous light, but with a low-pitched hum.

The room was coldly gray and largely vacant. Popov stood in front of a rectangular metallic intake table that spanned the length of a narrow room. Separated by wire mesh behind the table, stood rows of 3 by 3 feet steel cubicles, stacked from floor to ceiling, secured by heavy locks. It could have been a morgue if not for the absence of dead bodies.

A loud bang caused Popov's eyeballs to shift leftward as his head turned. Behind him, a worker in white jump suit and cap had pulled down the handle on a steel door. Beads of sweat rolled down Popov's cheeks.

Now in front of Popov, behind the intake table, a second bearded worker placed a one square foot box into reinforced packaging with an attached biohazard sign.

"Endereco…correto, Señor?"

Popov turned around and looked at the clipboard. In the destination lines, the recipient was designated: Dr. Rex Lee, Genometrics Corporation.

Popov sighed and replied, "Correto."

• • •

It was a misty, drizzly moonless night in Rio, amplified by the dampness of nearby shipping docks. With a buzz, the double layer

R. CHAPMAN WESLEY

of surrounding security gates sequentially opened. Popov rushed from the building onto wet pavement. He hailed a yellow taxi and popped into the back seat.

Inside, dull transmuted streetlights shined upon a middle-aged black woman with sharp angular features in a white turban and flowing white dress. From the passenger rear seat, Popov thought to himself; she looked like a Nubian Nefertiti.

Her center console looked like a religious shrine. A silver cross with a crystal red rose at its center, hung from the rearview mirror. On the console, miniature statues of catholic saints and an African "loa" stood on a makeshift "altar."

Popov leaned forward, "Vamos a Petropolis. Fale ingles?" The Nubian replied, "Sim, Señor."

Popov sighed and closed his eyes. The woman looked at Popov through her rearview mirror. The muted light caused his olive cheeks to glisten; his silver beard seemed to sparkle. She turned on the ignition.

The bearded worker walked out of the facility and stood in the shadow of the security fence. As the taxi pulled away, he exited the fence, looked to his left, and nodded.

A block away, Liz, a slender, dark eyed young Asian woman with short-cropped black hair, lean in a skin-tight black leather body suit, sat on a black motorcycle. She smiled and nodded back. She put on a black tinted helmet, engaged her bike and waited until the yellow taxi turned right two blocks away, and then jetted off.

• • •

In the distance, the halo of Rio shined upward through tropical clouds over the peaked hills and mountains of the world's largest urban rainforest, vigilantly guarded by The Corcovado, Christ the Redeemer. The Nubian had made good time. But she was traveling toward a destination she could not have foreseen.

She looked over the steering wheel. The gas gauge read half. It would be enough to get her to Petropolis, but what about her return? In her favela, it was not easy raising a very bright daughter on a meager salary of one. She peered at a sleeping Popov through the mirror. The white-haired, white bearded old man seemed kindly. Surely, he would understand without her explaining. The sign was coming up.

She navigated the taxi up a curved access entrance to a combination gas station-convenience store-restaurant-rest stop.

The Nubian stopped and turned to the back seat. Popov, with his head against the passenger rear window, was still fast asleep. The Nubian whispered at first, then louder "Señor…Señor … Must have gas, Señor."

Popov stirred. Dazed, he looked out of the window then blinked on the gas gauge. He then focused on the cross and on the miniature statues that earlier while driving, seemed to dance on the console. Popov pulled out a 100 reis bill and smiled, "I believe that you are a profoundly honest, deeply spiritual person."

He handed her the bill. She smiled, took the bill, exited the taxi, and walked to the store entrance. Popov grinned. He appreciated her humble gratitude.

As she entered, Liz walked out past the Nubian and glided toward the taxi like a hungry mama panther with cubs to feed.

Popov grabbed the briefcase, popped it open, and frantically wrote on a piece of paper. He closed the briefcase, and with it, jumped out of the cab.

A black limo pulled around the back side of the store, circled around, and sped toward Popov. Popov ran toward the access road. A tour bus entered from the highway.

The Nubian exited the store. Popov stopped and looked at her. He then walked straight into the path of the oncoming bus. It crushed him. Passengers on the bus screamed hysterically. The briefcase and its contents were strewn across the highway.

The Nubian froze into a column of stone. Liz halted and turned. The limo backed up to her. She entered. The limo sped off. A crowd of horrified onlookers circled Popov's mangled body.

The Nubian got in her taxi and quickly drove off.

• • •

The yellow taxi wound its way up a two-lane highway into the thickest part of the favela. It stopped far short of a bungalow with corrugated aluminum-stainless steel coverings. Still shocked, the Nubian leaned over, rested her arms on the steering wheel, and fought back tears, welling, but not spilling from her eyes.

She had been frightened. Now, she was dumbfounded. What had just happened?

Now it was very late. Her young daughter was wiser than she could ever have hoped. But hunger has a way of mitigating reason. And guilt cannot assuage a mother's obligation. She looked to the window; her daughter was not looking for her. She hoped she was asleep. The Nubian slowly pulled the taxi into a carport.

The Nubian got out. A glint in her eye, something in the back seat. She opened the back door and picked up a handwritten note. Under it, she saw bundles of $100 dollar bills. She gasped. She looked around and then quickly stashed the cash in her dress.

Something else! Something shiny under the passenger seat. She reached down and pulled out an amulet necklace with a central green crystal.

CHAPTER 6

DOCTOR LEE

"Why create death...?"

The first day of actual combat. Finally, theory would be applied; objective thought previously visualized, would now be transformed into action. It was central to Wong's instruction...to sustain the inner confidence of always being one step ahead. Constantly, the master had expounded this; as well as the danger of...distraction.

No thing; no transfer of gravity, no hand, no foot, nothing, no conscious action can be quicker, more forceful, more penetrating than subconscious mind.

Daylight was shunned; the Dojo's arena had no windows. The flame of four candles flickered muted light to the center, where Wong in red silk, and eyes closed, stood with his back to Rex. Though primed to attack, Rex, with bronze skin, in black silk, stood respectfully, waiting for a sign that would not come... Wong's ploy to instill initiative.

With suddenness, Rex raced forward. It was over before it began.

Alternating with pointed feet, Rex's open hands formed into fists, flashed and then whisked through black sleeves at multiple elusive points of Wong's body. Wong's palms from red silk sleeves parried away both fists and feet.

A single upward palm strike sent Rex parallel, thudding onto a gray mat. Wong turned on the overhead lights. The walls of the dojo had the usual assortment of martial arts weapons; "numb chucks," spiked balls, bamboo sticks, etc. Rex rested on his elbows, looked upward, and managed a self-deprecating smile. Wong, as calm and fatherly as ever, stood above him.

"You know, Rex, defend can be attack," Wong said sternly. He laughed to himself, and then smiled broadly. "Rex, you want me call you 'Grasshopper?'"

Wong gestured Rex to rise and walked to the other side of the room. Rex followed Wong to a miniature waterfall, tinkling into a ceramic pan. Wong picked up a silver chop stick and swirled it in the water.

"Nothing can be written into water."

Although knowing time was limited, Wong expounded further.

"Most people … like sand on beach. Stick come along and write into them. Effect last for short time. Soon wind blow, tide rise, and sand become smooth again. Other, like stone. Something hard carve into them. No wind, no tide, nothing change them. Very few like Living Buddha. Buddha like unending river of vibrant feeling. Nothing can be written into river."

Rex hears, then sees his phone, vibrating across the room. His lesson was over.

Rex placed his left palm over his right fist and bowed to Wong. Wong reciprocated and waved his hands.

"Okay. You go now."

· · ·

It was refreshing for Rex to feel the light moisture of the Northern California ocean breeze on the sweaty roots of his soft black hair. He had removed his black helmet and thick black leather jacket. It yielded instant relief. Despite the proximity of his destinations, he had never taken the ocean side turn-off before. From the overlook, he descended accommodating rocks to the mid-point of the cliffs below.

Even though work was waiting for him, he had time. The experiment would submerge him deep into the night. Perhaps to some, a tedious night; to others, fruitless. But to him, it could be the final culmination, a steppingstone, not only to wealth and security, but also to self-vindication, forged by the zeal to prove the naysayers wrong.

Besides, she would not be home waiting for him. He so much wanted her to be so. He so much wanted her in every way.

Rex looked to the soon setting sun. It descended into a distant cloud layer. Its light fractioned into echoes of mid-ocean waves, sand-less beach, and the curvy bay cliff coastline, lined with redwoods.

Across the small bay stood Genometrics. He had never seen it like that before, structures of ultra-modern Japanese design, conglomerates of glass, steel, and stone, shiny or dull, depending on the sun's angle. From here, the entire complex was quartz-like and naturalistic, except for the hardened barriers placed below the cliffs at the ocean's edge.

He began his climb. The sun had set. So far, this picturesque day had not gone as intended. But how lucky was he to find so near, a master of the hard style, who, as far as he knew, had never taken a student.

He arrived at his aerodynamic superbike. He slapped thick headphones over his helmet. There would be no cops on this road. He engaged the bike and jetted off through the wind tunnel of redwoods that lined the two-lane highway.

• • •

Already past the guard gate, the web of security, and external parking, Rex cruised to the circular curve that serviced both business and research facilities. He parked his bike along red stripes that signaled "no parking." Unexpectedly, the door of the research facility swung open.

Ahead at an entry desk sat Atlas Bosch, 55 and fit, a good-natured Appalachian veteran of unspeakable man-made crises. In their past, his seldom seen face had morphed into every frame of emotion, the kind of familiarity that bonds men together while others die in the mud around you.

Rex approached, "What the hell are you doing here?"

Atlas shrugged, "Not the only one. Lots of new faces. You'd think I'd be the one to know, wouldn't you?"

Atlas then flashed his badge: "Head of Security."

"Damn, Brother! Saving mankind can't wait a day?"
"Absolutely not. You of all people should know that by now."

• • •

The research elevator zoomed. Govinda's lab was a long way down, deeply imbedded in reinforced steel, concrete, and lead casings… necessary measures to shield the facility from the reactor if a release of radiation, much less the unthinkable, a meltdown, should occur.

Deceleration to the reactor level was abrupt and momentarily subtracted 20 pounds of "g" from the average person and a wave of nausea from the less hearty. The elevator doors slid open like metallic curtains.

Rex made his way through the circular hallway. After passing the reactor control room, he entered the lab after swiping his access badge below a red sign: "Radio-Virology Laboratory" with warnings in multiple languages: "Actung; Streng Verbotten."

Popov's proposal to insert radioactive isotopes into viral genes had been a conceptual breakthrough. According to his theory, after incorporating radioactive viral genes, cancer cells would no longer be able to secrete protein disguises and hide from immune cells. Govinda championed the concept. But it had been Rex's grunt work, as a lowly research fellow, that had created the therapeutic promise.

The small office adjacent to the enclosed experimentation space was modest, but it was his. Govinda rarely showed up. When he did, Govinda was more "thumbs" than "hands," great on pontification, light on execution.

Over time, it was all right. Rex always took the initiative, completing college on a GI bill, med school and residency under a naval contract, and fellowship at NIH. It was his way. He just despised the stealing.

Everything was the same, except for a small box on a corner shelf. He raised it up and underneath found the manifest label: "Universal Shipping, Rio de Janeiro. Extreme Biohazard. Handle with Extreme Care." He tore off the plastic covering.

"To: Rex Lee, MD;"

"From: Professor Anatoly M. Popov."

"Popov?" He muttered. He hadn't heard from him in years. Why now?

Rex opened the desk drawer and observed a plaque: "Lieutenant Rex Lee, MD: Distinguished Young Investigator Award, National Institutes of Health," and a picture of Rex in a naval officer's dress uniform, holding the plaque and shaking hands with Popov. Standing next to them was Govinda, an impressive East Indian man in a dark three-piece suit.

• • •

Weeks later, Rex was planning the crucial experiment when he heard footsteps. In walked Professor Harold Govinda, 65, a blend of Brahman certitude with a Cambridge education.

Always in a hurry, Govinda got to the point, "Any progress?"

"If we're talking viral toxicity, not much."

"Did you modify my methods?" Rex ignored him and examined his log.

"You didn't even try?" Rex put the log down and looked squarely into Govinda's prying eyes, "Following a hunch."

"Doctor Lee, may I remind you, your job, the reason you're here, is to create a plethora of viral toxins."

Govinda was on edge. Pressure was coming from somewhere. If threatening Rex wouldn't work, maybe pleading might.

"Rex, we need to understand these viruses in order to best defend against them."

One thing about Rex, in the past he might have been inexperienced; but he never lacked confidence. And he knew Govinda was deficient in technical skills.

Rex leaned back in his armchair, "Well, Professor, I've been thinking. Maybe there's a better way. Why create death? Then seek a means to contain it?"

• • •

A glistening liquid drop slowly expanded. The droplet hung on the tip of a glass pipette, then gently splashed into a circular Petri dish. Enclosed in a helmeted suit, Rex sat in a separate cubicle and peered through thick clear leaded glass. A robotic arm moved the circular dish into an incubation slot, marked "Cancer #44-2974"

• • •

The shower spray had been intense; the steamy mist refreshing. Now in the shower room with towel around his waist, Rex stared into the mirror at his slim, but well defined muscular upper torso and mixed-race face…of which races, it did not matter.

Rex closed his eyes, bent his knees, and held an "invisible ball" over the center of his body. It was now time for Tai Chi, the soft style used only by the most accomplished of masters for defense.

Rex "parted the horse's mane," "spread the white crane's wings," "brushed knees and pushed," "played the flute," "retreated and repulsed the monkey," "held the Chi," "grasped the bird's tail," and "rolled the single whip."

Rex held the pose, then stood straight up.

A short time later, in his white lab jacket, wearing his thick headphones, Rex looked through a binocular microscope. He pulled back, somewhat stunned. He processed the data on his computer and created a time lapsed video of microscopic cellular action and projected it onto a large screen.

Stained cancer cells, imbedded in a matrix of translucent normal cells, divided aggressively then crowded out and killed the normal cells. Immune florescent white cells were introduced, but nothing happened. But then Rex's viral particles were introduced and attached themselves to the immune cells. Within seconds, the immune cells were no longer blinded. The immune cells gobbled up and killed the cancer cells.

It was potentially a revolutionary discovery. Rex now reasoned that this particular virus could induce immune cells to attack ANY type of cancer. Previously, the focus had been on viral targeting of specific types of cancers cells.

Rex flashed a broad smile. He took off the headphones and flipped a switch on an amplifier. Overhead speakers blared out

"The Notorious B.I.G," 90s Gangsta Rap…just the beat without the lyrics, his precaution against an unannounced visitor. Frenetically, Rex danced alone to the funk.

CHAPTER 7

GIA

The clear night sky was a cold dark blanket, sprinkled with a sheen of starry crystals. Below on the flat Chilean plateau, only what the crescent moon allowed, was seen. Dim moonlight reflected off 66 circular funnels, neatly aligned in rows, all aiming their antennas to a single point of sky. At over 16,000 feet, the air was so thin that maintenance workers of the Atacama Large Millimeter Array radio telescope field, wore masks pressurized with supplemental oxygen.

Daytime, the plain was so dry and red it looked like Mars. But it was deep night when Doctor Gia Marina Lee, PhD could do her best work, searching for evidence of exo-planetary oxygen. Such data, she believed, would point the direction to finding extraterrestrial life.

But working alone had other advantages. She was, without question, the "hottest" astrobiologist that any male scientist had ever seen. While she was quite adept at fending off unwanted prurient interest, she had other things on her mind.

Why had Rex not called?

Rex was the only man she had ever loved; the only man who listened deeply and melded with her feelings in a unifying dream.

Could there be another? She felt not. But who can resist errant thoughts when the mind is consumed by a vacuum?

She started to reflect.

In many ways Rex was still an enigma. But he had always been honest. Bells of clarity rang in his words from the first instant of their meeting.

At that time, she resided in the deepest emotional dungeon of her 23 years; a crisis worse than the divorce of her well-to-do father from her mother and exile to the favela, worse than her mother's death from metastatic breast cancer, worse than the attempted assault by her uncle, her mother's brother.

From the depths of her despair, she was rescued, raised, schooled, and nurtured by Tia Lucia, her father's elder sister, who overwhelmed Gia with profound love and affection. But now her father had died suddenly. Lucia's assets were frozen, embroiled in an inheritance dispute with the jealous second wife.

Was Gia now about to have to sell herself…to take steps toward a sordid destination from which she could not return?

She was, by her account, a virgin. Of course she had boyfriends, but nothing had ever come of it, nothing beyond the heaviest of petting. Her voluptuous body at age 16 and the attention of boys had driven her middle-aged uncle into a supplemental, synthetic testosterone rage. However, unlike before, Lucia could not rescue her. And now, she could not ask more of Lucia.

Still absorbed in her memories, Gia sat down at her desk and stared at the phone. She started to tap her fingers on the desk but then stopped. Sighing, she closed her eyes and continued her reflection.

. . .

KNOCK. KNOCK.

The sound was firm but respectful. It stirred an alertness, but she did not open her eyes. She squinched.

KNOCK. KNOCK. Now more insistent.

"Gia," a firm female voice rang out.

Mama had seen this before. She had assured Gia that Gia would come to no harm. The termos, (a place of secret sexual encounters) had its reputation to protect, an obligation to its garotas (the prettiest of girls) and to its visiting men of substance. But it was all based on the prices the termos could charge.

Gia blurted out that she had vomited. But Mama wasn't having it. She paid particular attention to the first night of any new girl. To her, Gia had looked perfectly well.

Gia, in a private bathroom stall, opened her eyes and realized that she was holding on to a silver locket around her neck. Opening the locket, she looked at a heart-shaped photograph of her elderly white-haired Lucia. She closed the locket, detached it, and placed it into the side pocket of her tight jeans.

She stood up from a turned down toilet cover and opened the stall door.

In front of her, in the women's restroom of the most elegant gentleman's club in Rio de Janeiro, the eyes of Mama, the 57-year-old mama-san, peered at Gia, perturbed but then soothing and accepting.

Mama reached out and pulled Gia into an arm-circling embrace.

• • •

Although the L-shaped stairway, like the hallway, was narrow, Mama walked down the stairs arm in arm with Gia.

"Our clients are among the best in Rio," she said. "And, for that reason, perhaps the best in the world. Just take your time, Dear. Of course, do what feels comfortable. You'll be fine."

At the landing, Gia stopped the descent and looked directly into Mama's eyes.

Mama shrugged.

"Just do what comes naturally."

They reached the next floor. Mama opened a door and walked Gia inside.

The dark walled room was full of attractive young garotas, women of multiple hues, mostly in their 20s, but some up in their 40s, at various stages of changing from casual street attire to scant coverings, designed to reveal their individual enticements.

At bulb-encircled mirrors, voluptuous garotas were at various stages of prepping themselves with rouge and high gloss.

Tapping the wall to get their attention, Mama announced,

"This is Gia. Let us show our manners."

The girl sitting next to the door looked up and smiled.

The two girls at the far side of the room glanced over at Gia and then smiled at each other.

Some feigned disinterest. One older woman, past her prime, squinted and curled her lips.

As Mama left, the girl next to the door shooed another to move aside and gestured for Gia to sit down. Gia nodded and attempted a smile for the first time, then turned reluctantly toward the mirror. The remaining girls, almost all universally friendly but quickly disinterested, sat nearby and continued their prepping.

Gradually, the dimly lit room emptied of thinly clad women, descending to the bar below, excited, neutral, or detached, for the prospect of a night of familiar and/or anonymous sex, later to be heard fully engaged in audible passionate moans in rooms above.

Gia would be the last to leave and not easily at that. She sat in the dressing room alone, staring at herself in the mirror.

KNOCK, KNOCK, KNOCK. Gia did not respond.

The door squeaked slightly open.

Mama's voice rang out.

"Don't you think it is time to come down now, Sweetheart?"

• • •

The bar was full of young women competing for the attention of men uniformly dressed in white terry cloth bathrobes, devoid of cell phones and valuables, safely secured in lockers on floors below. When the access door opened, and as she stood at the threshold of the bar's entry, time froze. Every eye focused on her statuesque frame.

Internally awkward as she entered, she nevertheless projected the grace of a prima ballerina. Every male eye was enticed by the sway of her bottom. One vodka-drinking, young carioca, (a native male of Rio) nudged his friend with an elbow and said, "Ela chegou chegando." Or "She arrived, arriving."

Some enlisted navy non-coms from the southern fleet's annual docking, emitted "oohs" and "ahhs."

A couple of girls blunted the stares of horny older men by shunting her to the bar.

From there, Gia saw Rex for the first time. He was sitting among the sailors who had dragged "The Doc" away from his dock-side labors. Rex was sandwiched between a carnival-quality blonde and a stunning half-black, half-white mulita, both competing for his attention.

When two young inebriated cariocas approached Gia with offers of drinks, Gia shocked herself. Politely refusing, she walked across the room, stood directly in front of Rex, and asked him, in perfect English, to buy her a drink.

He looked up, smiled, and said in remarkably good Portuguese. "O que voce bebe?" ("What do you drink?")

Gia replied, "Thank you so much, sir. You are very kind. I would very much enjoy a Pepsi-cola."

Both girls sitting beside Rex answered in unison, "Aqui tem somente Coke!" ("Here they have only Coke.")

They all laughed. Rex invited Gia to sit down.

The blonde looked behind Rex's head to the mulita.

The mulita winked and nodded her head. Sliding on the seat cushion, the blonde invited Gia to sit down next to Rex.

Rex looked into Gia's face and smiled broadly.

• • •

There in the bar, Rex and Gia then entered into several hours of animated, spirited discussion of a wide range of subjects. Others in their proximity gradually floated away from their self-enclosed bubble.

During this time, men and women randomly engaged each other in conversation, and, with sufficient attraction, retired upstairs to couple in loudly audible passion, only to return, to drink, or if enough time had elapsed and funds were plentiful, re-engage with a different partner. To this, Rex and Gia were completely oblivious; that is until Mama suggested that perhaps they might retire upstairs to more fully experience each other.

• • •

The dimly lit upstairs suite with its own shower stall had a queen-size bed with white linen in front of a headboard to ceiling mirror that covered the entire back wall. Rex sat on the bed with overwhelming anticipation and as much patience as he could muster.

Rex's eyes surveyed the room. A ceiling mounted AC unit spanned a sidewall. Next to the bed was a radio amplifier, and just beyond, hooks on the wall for hanging towels and robes.

When Rex heard the door lock click, he leaned back on the bed resting on his elbows. But as Gia entered, he sat up in rapt attention. Appearing cool seemed all too unnecessary.

She entered in a black see-through negligee wrap, which poorly disguised abundant sculptured curves, held firmly in a scarlet bikini.

Rex smiled and leaned back. She stood motionless. He just stared. Turning around, Gia raised her arms to untie the neck strings that held the negligee.

He rose and stood behind her. Gathering the detached strings, he slowly tied them back together, then gently held her shoulder and turned her around.

"You haven't done this before, have you?"

They looked into each other's eyes. She dropped her gaze. Smiling, he tenderly guided her to the bed, but gestured for her to sit.

"I want to know more; in fact, I want to know everything about you."

From a bowed head, she raised her eyes.

"Perhaps, you feel the same?" He continued. "You can ask me anything...seriously."

She held up her right hand in a fist and extended her right pinky finger.

"Pinky Swear?" He asked.

"Truth or dare!" She replied.

"Truth! Dares can come later."

She smiled. She pointed to his glass.

"You drink only...water?"

"No, I can choose. But let's just say I like being healthy."

"Why? Are you a doctor?"

"Well, as a matter of fact, I am."

She smiled.

He pointed to her glass.

"Why only Coke?"

"Well, Doctor, that is only for tonight. Besides, Pepsi, remember?"

He shook his head. "Yes, of course...Pepsi. Pepsi?"

"Let us just say...I take the Pepsi challenge!"

He laughed. "So now you're a comedian?"

She feigned being stern, smiled, formed a fist, and lightly punched him in the left shoulder. Then she laughed outright.

"And you knew there was no Pepsi here?"

"Of course." She nodded. "Tem somente Coke aqui!" ("There is only Coke here!")

At that point, Rex was reticent to couple with her. He found her childlike innocence endearing and expressed a respectful affinity for her that they both had never experienced before. He wanted to know everything about her. Of course, she told him of her hardships, but he wanted to know her dreams.

She shared with him childhood wanderings on vacant beach and through rainforest adjacent to the favela, about the quiet times of deep night to watch stars and speculate about their origins and about the unseen people and animals that must live there. She explained her fascination with numbers and abstract mathematics, which seemed to be written into the synchronistic fabric of the universe. It was then that he realized that she was the smartest woman that he had ever known.

They kept talking on and on, enrapt in each other. Rex kept upping their time in the suite, right up to the time of closure.

Finally, the wall phone gave off a short repetitive buzz.

"10 minutes... Then we must go," she told him.

He looked at his watch.

"Got to go anyway," he replied.

"You come back to see me tomorrow?"

He nodded.

"Early?"

"Yes, I'll come back for you."

She extended the pinky of her right hand.

"Pinky Swear?"

His pinky embraced hers. They shook. Their eyes locked upon each other. He rose.

As she rose, she formed a fist and lightly punched towards his left shoulder. He deflected away her fist, turned her forearm over, and gently planted a kiss on her right inner wrist. He then looked up and smiled.

When they left the building, Rex promised that he would return at the opening of the very next day.

• • •

The next day, unlike the day before, Gia relished her return to the termos. She was filled with an overwhelming anticipation to see Rex again.

An analog clock on the dressing room wall noted 3 PM.

In the dressing room alone, with her face in the mirror, Gia finished the last application of rouge. The mulita entered but abruptly stopped and smiled when she saw Gia. Gia wore a stylish white negligée with a 2-piece traditional white bikini beneath it.

• • •

From the bar entrance, Gia peaked inside a cracked door. The bar was half full with guys and girls. An American man approached her from the hallway behind. He politely excused himself as she stepped aside. She forced a smile but then, after he passed, she shook her head.

• • •

Gia reclined in the most distant lounge chair in a vacant unisex relaxation lounge. Above a TV showing a Brazilian soap, a digital clock displayed 8 PM.

• • •

In the reception area at the entrance, Gia stood in front of a desk where patrons were lined up to either enter or pay as they left.

The male receptionist explained to her in Portuguese, "No, he is not with another girl. He did not come in."

• • •

At a corner barstool pushing 11 PM, Gia sat as far away from customers as she could, intentionally shielding herself with idle girls in front of her.

A grotesquely obese European "frequent flyer," known for being particularly over-bearing, nudged the girls in front of Gia aside and stood directly in front of her.

"What do you say? Let's you and I have a little drink!"

Gia got up and walked out of the bar.

Now, the confrontation with Mama was inevitable.

• • •

In the girl's locker room adjoining the restrooms, Gia found that her combination lock had been replaced.

Mama walked in.

"You cannot just come here and act like you own this place. Like it is your own personal little playground."

Mama moved closer and loomed over Gia.

"Who do you think you are, anyway?"

Gia stood up and got right in Mama's face.

"Gia!"

Gia stormed out.

• • •

Gia stood in her negligée outside of the club as neighborhood people walked by and stared at her.

She saw a small sandwich/coffee shop with seats and tables about 50 yards away across the street at the corner. She walked towards it.

Later, as untouched, cold coffee sat on the table before her, Gia folded her arms across her chest and shivered.

Just hours before closing, the mulita walked out of the club in street clothes. Looking around, she saw Gia at the coffee shop. She walked toward Gia, carrying something.

When she reached Gia, she opened a bag and took out a long white bathrobe. A tear ran down Gia's left cheek as she stood up and hugged the mulita. The mulita smiled and placed the bathrobe around her shoulders.

Still later, Gia laid with her head on the table, eyes closed, and her face turned toward the club.

Rex walked behind 3 animated navy guys along the street toward the club's entrance. One guy looked back at Rex, who was walking with his eyes down and carrying something.

At the entrance of the club, the 3 guys enthusiastically entered. Rex hesitated. He saw a trash can near the door and pondered it.

Just as Rex was about to pass through the threshold into the club, Gia saw him, jumped to her feet, and waved.

"Rex! Rex!"

No response. Rex entered.

She plopped back down into the chair, laid her head on the table, wrapped her arms around her head, and sobbed. After 5 minutes, Gia gathered herself and stood up. She tied the robe around her waist, wiped the tears from her eyes, and walked down the sidewalk. She raised her hand to hail a cab.

"Gia!"

She turned to see Rex across the street, waving a bouquet of red roses over his head.

"Hi, Sweetheart! I thought you might be needing these."

Rex had been delayed by an unexpected shipboard traumatic injury.

She smiled and ran across the street, barely avoiding oncoming traffic in both directions.

Gia sailed into his arms. It was a hunger neither had ever before experienced.

As their lips met and their tongues danced around each other, an energy welled upward and expanded beyond the space between their ears, connecting them soul to soul. After the kiss that sealed them forever, there was nothing left to say. They entered the nearest hotel and made love all night.

• • •

Suddenly, the phone rang, startling Gia out of her deep reverie. She picked up. Rex could have sung the words.

"Honey, I miss you so much. Sorry for all that I put you through. Please come back now. I love you."

Gia, with tears in her eyes responded, "Oh, Rex. I'll come soon."

CHAPTER 8

REFUSAL OF THE CALL

When Rex's discovery leaked out through the corporate net-work, the company's stock skyrocketed. The accolades to Rex came quickly as did Govinda's consternation. The implications for Genometrics were enormous.

A consensus was emerging; there was a greater than 87% prob-ability that Rex may have discovered a universal cure for all can-cers. To some, it was just a matter of testing. After having gotten private assertions from leading scientists in their fields, the CEO, Alexi Vitkin, the portrait of effortlessly acquired wealth through questionable means, decided to divulge the data to hedge fund managers and their consultants, rather than the traditional route of peer-reviewed publication.

While Govinda agreed, Rex did not. It was a new footnote in the litany of their disagreements, inevitably to be fought out over patent rights. Govinda, though difficult, had always been direct. But now he was surprisingly absent as if somehow restrained.

The big day had arrived.

In the reception area of a ballroom, well-heeled, big-time investors milled around, sipped incredibly expensive wine, lined up deals, and bubbled with an enthusiasm rarely displayed in a crowd of extremely rich people.

Vitkin, 50 and vital, entered the room with Liz on his arms. She sported a white pants suit with angel wing sleeves, an open back, and a V breast line, held together by a diamond studded VR brooch. She wore a broad, floppy white hat with black brim; black stiletto "fuck me harder" high heels; and "cat woman" glasses with opaque yellow lenses.

Following the shockwave, applause broke out, followed by an "all smiles" rush to greet them; all except for a short, pale, bald white man, who held back and studiously examined the company's financial prospectus.

While this hobnobbing was going on, Rex found himself pimping his naval dress uniform in front of an ornate mirror in the most luxurious bathroom of the most expensive hotel room he had ever stayed in. He had only marginally agreed to the presentation. And then it happened. His cell phone on the counter, set on silence, vibrated. After weeks of no communication, Govinda!

Why now? It was all he could take.

• • •

There was high tension in the ballroom. Low pitched murmurs rumbled through the crowd. On stage was a conference table for three with placards in front. Govinda sat stone-faced with arms bound tightly across his chest. Vitkin rested his knee on the table. The fingers of his right hand tapped the table rhythmically but impatiently. The chair behind the placard, "Commander Rex Lee, MD," was empty.

In large letters, the screen behind the podium projected: "Genometrics: The World Leader in Universal Cure."

Vitkin looked at Liz. He nodded. She got up and left the room.

• • •

The echoes of his leather boots reverberated through the long underground access tunnel of the plush San Francisco hotel. To his surprise, waiting at the end in front of a service elevator, was Atlas spiffed out in an Italian business suit.

As Rex arrived wearing his black leathers, Atlas belted out.

"Ain't you still on loan from 'The Man'? Homie, you be going the wrong way!"

Rex smiled and rubbed his thumb and index finger through Atlas' coat lapel.

"That sham show? Hmm. Your last day? A bit out of your element, wouldn't you say?"

"My Man, that's some touché. Got an anonymous text… today. Said you was the 'Bleep.' Yo Bro, you the 'Bleep'?"

The two went from a fist bump to a palm clasp to a forearm bash and finished with their tongues wagging out.

• • •

Rex exited the roof top parking garage elevator carrying his black helmet. Only two vehicles were in sight; his superbike and a black, heavily tinted Cadillac Escalade parked near the down ramp.

But Rex should have seen what he could not see. He was being telescopically observed.

Several blocks away from the vantage of a high hotel suite, Yan Chou, about 32, a clean shaven, buttoned down dapper Chinese dude, too fit to conceal his cat-like reflexes, observed Rex through a tripod-based telescopic camera. Yan looked down at his silver digital watch and pointed his index finger downward.

Well behind an adjacent window, Shih, age 60, a tall slender Chinese man with steely eyes and an angular face, projected a parabolic funnel toward the garage and pushed "enter" on a laptop.

A computer monitor registered #444666; time: 09:44 AM, Beijing time. Above the case number and time signature, an analog voice tracing fluctuated. The computer speaker spewed forth a thick German accent.

"Doctor Lee, a word, if you please?"

Rex watched a lanky bald man with thick bifocals exit the passenger side of the SUV.

"Doctor Werner Ehrlich, Heisenberg Institute."

The window of the driver's seat rolled down. The driver's hand flashed a badge, "Tom Stern. CIA."

Rex took a seat in the back. Nothing was said for about a minute after the windows shut. Then the two men turned in unison to Rex. Rex took the initiative.

"OK, gentlemen. I have not seen my wife in months."

Stern smirked, "Dead…lines. Everybody's got one."

Ehrlich shook his head and looked again to Rex, "Doctor Lee, you worked under Professor Govinda, is it so?"

"More like collaborated. Actually, I don't work under anybody or anyone." Ehrlich nodded, approvingly; the "Kid" has "cajones."

Impatient, Stern broke in, "Well, ever collaborated on 'Rising Fever?'"

"Never heard of it."

"The viral sample. How'd you get it?"

"Popov. About 4 weeks ago."

"We know about your award. Any unregistered collaborations? Social interactions or business dealings outside the lab?"

Rex shook his head.

"Tried to reach him, didn't you? Multiples times."

Rex was getting testy.

"What the "f" is this about?"

"From a clandestine lab, Popov steals the deadliest virus known to man, alters it, and sends it to you. Despite a very public suicide in Rio, his identity and any traces of him being in Rio go white-washed by embarrassed Brazilian intelligence. Of course, we knew."

Rex rolled back in the seat and stared out of the window.

"Now a novice virologist, such as yourself, makes an incredible, Earth-shattering breakthrough. Well, questions are asked. And we want answers."

Rex had had enough. "Nothing! Got nothing for you. Got it! I'm out of here."

Rex bolted. Stern grimaced. Ehrlich retorted. "Let him go. He wants to get laid. Surely, you can remember that."

CHAPTER 9

GOVINDA

"Oi...Gostoso!"

With headphones crackling in his ears, Rex churned his superbike around curve after curve of ocean cliffs. As he drove, he loved to rap aloud to hip hop lyrics, and "Hip Hop Away" by "Naughty by Nature" was no exception.

Too funky, too fast, he hit gravel on a tight curve, skidded, and nearly wiped out on a column of trees. He regained control, smiled, and motored on.

• • •

Rex parked his bike in front of their quaint modern two-story glass and steel house, whose back faced the ocean cliffs. The front door was slightly ajar. He pushed it open slowly without announcing his arrival. Over time, he had learned not to disrupt any trap that she might be setting.

He walked down the short hallway into the living room. Sure enough, she had rearranged the furniture and mementos; her way of asserting her presence.

The framed photos were all on the mantle: Gia at 18, dancing in an "escola de samba," and two framed photos of Rex, in one, bowing to Master Wong, and in the other, standing with a platoon of Navy Seals.

The small bronze statuette of a voluptuous naked girl was now on the bar. Dark wooden African masks on an isolated red wall were now asymmetrically arranged. A Greek icon of Saint George slaying the dragon was propped up on the coffee table. Religious motifs, a menorah and a large Islamic mandala, were now on a distant table next to a 5-foot-tall standing wooden Thai Buddha with outstretched palms pointing down.

Alone, unmoved on an adjacent wall was a crucifix with Christ facing downward.

Rex meandered into a nook next to the kitchen. The table was replete with; lit candles, a small basted roasted turkey, pre-pulled Jamaican jerky, cranberry sauce, candied yams, collard greens, creamed corn, sautéed spinach, puffed biscuits, deviled eggs, assorted wine glasses, a chilled bottle of Rombauer Chardonnay, and two glasses (one slightly sipped) of '97 Sawyer Reserve Cabernet. It was a feast for a King.

She was an accomplished, highly respected scientist, but more importantly, a ravishing Brazilian woman, who knew what she liked, and what Rex had come to like.

Rex sat down at the head of the table and stared at the place card, "Admiral Rex." Suddenly from the kitchen, a rheostat dimmed the overhead lights…

Gia exited the kitchen wearing a circular white sailor's cap and an American flag tonga bikini, covered by a chef's apron. She stood in front of him, "Admiral Rex, very bad. You are late. The food is done, and the oven is already cooling."

Rex pointed to her seat. "Where is your place setting?"

Gia pulled aside the top of her apron and revealed the curvature of her breast and a badge, "Gia."

She smiled, "I'm the chef. And I can sit wherever I want."

She turned and walked into the kitchen. Her backless apron exposed the mounds of her bottom, separated only by a bikini cord.

She re-entered with a small bowl of pudding. She plopped her bottom down on his lap and picked up a spoon. He smiled. She wagged her index finger in front of his lips.

"No, no, no."

She placed the spoon on the table.

"That's not the way to start dessert!"

She dipped her index finger into the bowl, swirled out some pudding, put it between his lips, then bent over into a tongue-filled kiss.

• • •

The creaking of wood against wood emanating from the floor above, began again.

The lights were still dimmed. The white table cloth, stained red. Candle wax had spread at the base of still lit, nearly melted candles.

An apron, bikini top and bottom, and black leathers were strewn over bamboo floor. Between their passions, someone had been eating. A quarter of the food had been consumed.

The creaking of wood over wood grew louder, faster.

The voice of Gia rang out,

"Aah… Querido!"…"Oi…Gostoso…Que delicia!... Me Foda… Foda mi buceta!"

Faster, more insistent!

"Aah, Marido…Faca!...Me faca!... Vai, Amor!... Vai!"

• • •

The midnight moon hung high above and shone down upon the oak deck that projected from their master bedroom. Below, slow waves rolled in. High tide had narrowed the beach.

With his back against the deck railing, Rex looked through open bay doors to Gia's curved, sleeping body, entwined in soft bedding. He turned back to the ocean, perplexed by many questions.

Popov dead? By suicide? A virus linked to bioterrorism? Even he, an astute virologist, after further altering the virus, had no inkling.

Alterations of the original strain had to have been profound! An intuitive flash, his wild hunch, based on Popov's old data, had led to an unforeseen discovery. What was Popov's true intent?

In his core, he began to feel it. A vast darkness was gathering.

"Aaagh," Gia's voice rang out.

Rex rushed through the bay doors. Gia was cowering against the headboard. She pointed to thick throw rug at the foot of the bed. A large cockroach laid on its back with its legs upward, flailing. Rex grabbed a bell jar covering an antique microscope. He slid a piece of paper under the roach, covered it with the jar, inverted it, carried it to the railing, and dumped the roach over the side.

Gia exclaimed, "Why? Why you let as baratas live?

Rex shouted, "Sou um doutor...medico. People, animals, plants, even things can die. I don't kill anything."

Gia smiled.

"Doctor! Always working. Why don't you come over and work some more on me?"

Rex sat beside her and lowered his head. She sat up and reached for his face.

"Suicide? This changes everything. Honey, I need you now more than ever." He held her at her waist.

There was never any real reason to have doubted him. Now, she was more curious than anything else.

"Darling, who is Erlinda Dos Santos?"

"Who?"

Gia reached under the side of the bed and dangled the necklace with the green amulet in front of him.

"From Rio to Chile, days ago I received it, just before I came. She sent this to me...for you. And why just two days ago?"

Rex was dumbfounded. Gia continued.

"Does she know Popov?"

Rex was exasperated. "I have no idea."

Rex's smart phone vibrated. He picked it up and turned it toward her face: "Govinda."

Rex answered, "Really, Professor?"

Govinda's voice was labored. "What you did…no limitations."

"That's very kind of you, Professor."

"Rex, I must see you."

"I'm listening."

Govinda was breathing even harder, "The virus came from me."

"Where the hell are you?"

Govinda's voice, barely audible, was now obscured by static.

"Climbing down to the beach below you."

• • •

Through the deck telescope, Gia watched the two men below, standing face to face on the beach.

Govinda sighed, "Lust for power and recognition. How selfish of me?"

"If you expect sympathy, it ain't happening. Still, the master of manipulation. So, you sent me the virus?"

"Yes, it was Vitkin's plan for greater toxicity. No one anticipated a breakthrough. Except perhaps Popov."

Rex shook his head.

"Oh man. Come clean, Professor."

"I intercepted the package. Further altered the virus. Tried and failed for The Cure. The key element was still missing. Tried not to involve you. Now only you can make it right."

Govinda reached into his coat, pulled out a thumb drive, and handed it to Rex.

"This is the key to unlock Popov's Quest for *The Well*."

"*The Well*?"

Govinda winced and gasped with his mouth wide open. His pupils dilated. His eyes rolled up. His arms reached outward. He fell forward into Rex's arms. Rex embraced him and felt the handle of an imbedded knife over his shoulder. Rex removed his hand. The black handle contained a miniature gold dragon.

On the deck, Gia pulled back from the telescope and screamed.

Rex looked up. Gia looked down in horror. A black clothed ninja scrambled through small boulders up the steep cliff. Rex ran and ascended after the ninja. The ninja slipped. Rex gained ground. The ninja threw down a rock, just missing Rex's head.

Rex grabbed the ninja's right foot and twisted it violently. The ninja struck Rex's shoulder with his left foot. Rex slid backward but escaped plummeting to the beach.

The ninja continued the ascent, scaled a wooden fence bordering Rex's house, jumped on a bike, and vroomed away.

Rex ran into the house and found Gia cowering at the distant side of the bed. Rex shouted, "Honey... Honey, we've got to go now!"

She pleaded, "Why not wait for police?"

"Honey, police can't help. We're going to have to remain calm and think our way out of this together. Grab whatever you can think of. We have to go now!"

Gia rummaged through her desk, ran out of the front door, jumped onto the waiting bike, and clung hard to Rex's back as he rocketed off.

CHAPTER 10

REVELATION

"...meet out here?"

The closet was completely dark, purposefully devoid of all light. Gia was resistant, but now accepted his logic. Maybe there would be things on the thumb drive that she shouldn't know, that might put her into greater danger. Rex had to look alone.

Wong's laptop apparently had never been connected to the web. Rex used the light from his smart phone and fingers to find the port. He powered up the computer and plugged in the thumb drive.

The monitor flickered into action. From a background of stars, a tiny Earth progressively magnified to encompass the screen. As it spun on its axis, magnification further honed down on northwestern Brazil, to a topographical map of the Upper Amazon with latitudinal and longitudinal coordinates of a rectangular 10,000 square mile area.

Models of water molecules based on the presence of hydrogen versus deuterium and tritium (i.e., "heavy water") appeared. A color scheme from red to violet was then presented, designating the relative concentrations of water versus heavy water. The color scheme then overlaid the topographical map, pointing out regions where the concentrations of heavy water in naturally occurring ground water was higher than expected.

A video head shot of Popov, now a mindful man long gone, then appeared and spoke. It was if he was talking from the other side.

"Dr. Lee, My Toveresh (Comrade) in Spirit, I impel you to seek the Victory of Spirit over Matter, transported by an interstellar meteorite from the least dense region of galactic space. The fulfillment of the Ultimate Promise to heal everything and everyone. The Power of *The Well* ... from Ancient China, the Cauldron, the means to deliver it, both of which surpass my current level of understanding.

"I developed biological weapons during proxy conflicts of the Cold War. I defected, but my consulting work could not escape the multinational compromise of unauthorized research upon an unknowing public.

"Now Vitkin seeks the perfection of a bioweapon of unimaginable carnage, only made useful by a yet-to-be perfected antidote.

"Dr Lee, I charge you now to find the Source and unveil the Mystery. Only you can restore the Promise of *The Well* and prevent an existential human catastrophe."

• • •

The moon now hung further out above the westward ocean. The tide had receded. Ten feet away, soft waves still rolled toward a rigid pant leg. A chill was in the air.

Stern kneeled next to the body of Govinda and then looked up at Rex's well-lit house. Ehrlich stood nearby. With chopsticks in his gloved right hand, Stern opened Govinda's coat and probed a slit above the inside pocket. Ehrlich rubbed his gloved hands together.

But then, Stern didn't seem surprised. "Nothing. There's nothing there."

Ehrlich nodded. Stern reached for his cell phone; no signal.

They climbed the cliff slowly. After reaching the top, they walked down the road a quarter of a mile away from Rex's house and got into the SUV.

Stern sat in the driver's seat. He placed the chopsticks in a plastic wrapper. Taking off his gloves, he reached for his cell phone, now sitting in the cup holder. Disinterested, Ehrlich rested against the passenger window, nodding with his eyes closed. Stern shook his head.

"Evidence connecting the virus to 'Rising Fever?' We could have made that exchange anywhere. Why the hell did Govinda want to meet out here?"

Now awake, Ehrlich shrugged and turned squarely to face Stern. He leaned over the cup holder toward Stern and looked down. Stern looked down at his phone. Ehrlich whipped out a handgun in his gloved right hand and placed it against Stern's right temple.

BANG!

Blood and brains splattered on the driver's side window.

Stern's lifeless body slumped. Ehrlich placed the gun in an open glove compartment and closed it.

Getting out of the car, Ehrlich popped the trunk and pulled out a large black garden bag. He removed his clothes, placed them in the bag, and closed the trunk.

Now naked, with the bag slung over his shoulder, Ehrlich walked along the highway away from the house. The headlights of two black limousines approached from behind. The rear door of one opened; Ehrlich jumped inside. The limos sped away.

CHAPTER 11
COMRADES AND VILLAINS

"1, 1, 2, 3, 5...8"

With a solitary window at her back, Gia sat at a simple table and typed code on the keyboard of the "antique" laptop. The small bedroom with bare walls was modest except for black standing lacquer panels connected by hinges, embroidered with brilliant jade figurines, a tribute to both the taste of the owner and the skill of the artist.

On the monitor, Gia pulled up a topographical map of a high-lighted 10,000 square mile rectangle along the Rio Negro, a north-west branch of the Amazon, 1000 kilometers from Manaus near the Venezuelan border. This location was 800 kilometers north and east of Popov's highlighted rectangle, nestled closer to the Colombian border.

Rex walked into the room. He looked over her shoulder. Hugging her from behind, he kissed her neck.

"Got it?"

Gia replied, "Yes, got it, Darling. It's weaponized."

Gia unplugged the thumb drive, turned, and gave it to him. He held on to her fingers.

"Thanks, Honey. That's why I love you."

Rex smiled and exited the room. Gia turned back to the screen and stared blankly.

• • •

Rex entered the arena of the Dojo and approached Wong at the far side, standing and reading a large book, supported on a granite pedestal.

Wong looked up and spoke, "You asked of … *Well.*"

Wong pointed to a page, revealing a 6-line hexagram, divided into 2 trigrams of solid or broken lines from "The I Ching." The hexagram was designated 48. Below it was the Chinese character for Jing, *The Well.*

"Upper three lines… water; bottom three lines…wood."

Wong turned the page. It depicted daily life in eight exquisitely detailed ancient Chinese villages, arranged in a circle suspended on eight spokes of a wheel, with the Chinese character for Jing at the center.

"According…Lao Tzu, even though town … change, *Well* … unchanged. It is source of all sustenance, physical and spiritual. All draw from *Well.*

Rex nodded.

"Then it can only benefit the world and mankind." Rex hopefully proposed.

"Not exactly. If wrong choices made, if intent of man selfish, if his tools evil or inadequate, if rope too short, or jug break, *Well* bring Misfortune."

Rex took in a deep breath and sighed. His eyes fell upon the miniature waterfall.

• • •

The air was still and silent; the usual slight ocean breeze absent.

Only one already predisposed to listening intently could hear the soft shuffling of satin slippers, slushing across the bow of the roof. Only one predisposed to seeing could see the rise of the upper window.

Gia had remained fixed, seated in front of the computer, staring above it and into an uncertain future.

A black robed ninja jumped through the window, flashed across the room, and restrained her from behind. He placed a wetted cloth around her mouth and nose. She struggled helplessly with arms and legs flailing.

Rex entered the room. Upon seeing Gia in trouble, Rex reached around the wall, grabbed a spiked metal ball, and threw it into the left forearm of the ninja. The masked ninja winced. Rex punched him unconscious across the temple and secured Gia's release. He unmasked a middle-aged Japanese man with bilateral facial scars.

In the dojo arena, ninjas rushed in from the main door with swords drawn and surrounded Wong on three sides. With steel pipe, Wong engaged the first rusher, stepped aside, and swatted him on the back.

Two remaining ninjas attacked simultaneously. Wong avoided their thrusts, dropped down and with a circular swipe, disarmed and crippled both ninjas.

Rex entered the room and shielded Gia. Three more ninjas with swords entered and surrounded Wong. Wong motioned for Rex to stand back. With pipe in hand, Wong fended off the ninjas' fencing thrusts. He vaulted with pipe in hand and with a circular kick, knocked all three ninjas unconscious.

Ehrlich and two more ninjas entered from the bedroom. One grabbed Gia. Rex grabbed a "numb-chuck" off the wall and released Gia by smashing the head of the ninja.

The other ninja rushed Rex. They punched in close. Ehrlich drew a pistol. Gia screamed. Ehrlich aimed and fired. The bullet shredded the ninja's head covering and half of his head.

Ehrlich smiled and aimed at Rex. Wong avoided and struck the remaining ninja, then rolling on the floor, with a round kick, struck Ehrlich unconscious. Gia rushed into Rex's arms. Rex handed Gia off to Wong and planted the thumb drive in Ehrlich's breast pocket.

• • •

With two hands clenched on a weighted rock, Rex swung down and smashed the driver's side window of the black limousine. He reached in, popped the hood, and severed the ignition cord. He ran past the other disabled limousine to a "Big Ass" green truck.

Wong sat in the driver's seat next to Gia. She reached through the window for Rex. He took her hand. She smiled and fought back tears. Again, there was nothing left to be said. The stakes were high at every level. But she had overwhelming confidence in him. His words had never failed. And he swore he would return.

Rex ascended the truck bay, jumped onto his superbike, and roared away. The truck sped off in the opposite direction.

• • •

Vitkin stood next to Liz. Surviving ninjas lined up in the middle of the dojo. All remained masked except for the unmasked Japanese man with bilateral cheek scars. Ehrlich stood to their side.

Ehrlich turned and spoke to Vitkin, "Herr Vitkin, now we wait."

Disappointed, Vitkin was curt, "Really? Clarify."

Ehrlich shrugged; it was his favorite way to make a point. "Yes, we simply wait. Reveal himself… He will. I'm certain of it."

Vitkin nodded and turned to Liz.

"Mademoiselle, si vous plait."

Liz drew a gun and pressed the barrel to the unmasked Japanese man's temple. He winced. The bullet burrowed through his skull and erupted like a volcano from his ear.

Ehrlich smiled. Liz swiveled and fired a bullet into Ehrlich's forehead. Ehrlich fell back, lifeless, to the floor.

Vitkin was not happy. But, hmm, he thought… Besides being the best fuck of his grotesquely rich and powerful life, maybe she knew something he didn't. If so, that was too much power. Suspicion began to arise in him but so did the memory of his enjoyment.

"Not exactly what I wanted! Check him."

Liz opened Ehrlich's coat pocket and extracted the thumb drive. She stood and handed it to Vitkin. Vitkin nodded.

"All right. His share. Find them!"

Vitkin examined the thumb drive. He then crunched it under his heel and pulled out a micro-transmitter.

• • •

Circuitous to avoid detection, Rex crisscrossed secondary roads of California, meandered high desert plains of Nevada, and finally reached the mountains and valleys of southern Utah. Though dirt tired, Rex was juiced.

The arduous journey provided ample time to reflect. It was no secret that Atlas had all the skills. Atlas would be there for him. Rex was convinced of it.

It had not always been that way. When they first met, the tension between the two men had been uncomfortable. But declarations came quickly, followed by an immense respect based on the capabilities of each man. Such respect is the glue that binds men in battle, erasing all prior limits.

Now, there was no time to spare. Now, "the shit" had to happen quickly, and Rex had to chance it.

North of Cedar City, he exited a two-lane highway at the base of the Dixie National Forest and headed east. He had to obey the speed limit, but overall, the journey was reasonably fast, rolling along straight highway, buttressed by uncut grassy plains and evergreen mountains.

It was getting dark. Distracted and then fascinated by the zig zag motion of flashing fireflies, Rex almost missed the marker for the camouflaged route.

To the unschooled eye, the marker would seem random and of no significance. But Rex knew beforehand that the secret number was 6, not 6 itself, but the 6th number in a sequence of Fibonacci numbers; 1, 1, 2, 3, 5, … 8. At the 8th interval between groupings separated by 100 yards, he was to find a grouping of 6 randomly sized boulders.

When he found the grouping, he pulled aside heavy brush that obscured the path, then used the brush to obscure his bike. The path itself was overgrown and difficult to navigate. It had not been walked or climbed for a very long time.

Much further up, Rex felt a twinge in his gut and a tingling on his neck. Instincts and training kicked in. His approach up the path had been unannounced. Despite unwavering camaraderie, it was all very, very dangerous.

A little further up, Rex spied the faint outline of an unlit log cabin next to a "copter-filled" pad, etched out of a small clearing. He ducked for cover behind an evergreen. Rex looked ahead, behind, right and then left. He felt he was…being watched…not by some infra-red wizardry, but more like a spider when someone walks unexpectedly into a just-lit room.

Rex looked up. A dark figure sprang from a branch and wrestled him to the ground. Out of a nearby bush, a familiar figure leaped forward, with a gloved hand pulled back Rex's assailant.

"Whoa. Whoa," Atlas exclaimed.

The assailant got up. Rex turned over. Standing above him was a somewhat handsome white dude of 29 years with blonde hair, blue eyes, high cheek bones, and a modestly muscular, supple body. If he had been a little thinner, he might have been a runway "showboat" for someone's New York spring collection.

Rex rose and dusted himself off.

Atlas smiled. "Hmm. Let me guess. Gia?"

"No. Thought I might pony up here and greet you ladies," Rex replied.

"Oh yeah? A true gentleman," Atlas said to the man. And then to Rex, "May I present … The Gap."

Rex extended his right hand. And The Gap reciprocated.

Rex, "Cool."

Gap, "Same."

CHAPTER 12

"GONNA TO NEED MORE"

"How about 'The Killer'?"

The log cabin had a basement lined on all four walls with built-in shelves. Row upon row held a plethora of transportable armament:

Handguns, sniper rifles, AK 47s, AR 15s, Uzis, RPGs, grenades, bazookas, anti-tank missiles, mine sweepers, land mines, mortars, mortar shells, and, mounted on a table, a 50-caliber machine gun.

Atlas studied Rex as Rex ran his fingers and his eyes over items of interest.

"Still conscientiously objecting?" Atlas injected.

It seemed a reasonable question to put to the son of a remotely deceased, social crusading Episcopal minister. Rex examined a shotgun, pumped it, and placed it back on the rack. He then examined an Uzi.

"Not exactly."

He put down the Uzi and visually examined an AK 47, still in the rack. Rex had to ask.

"What's the story on The Gap?"

Atlas spoke with the inflection of a proud dad.

"Vetted, 'Dark Water' sanctioned, Boy Wonder slash Robin

without a Batman in Afghanistan."

"Yeah, still can't see what you see in that bitch."

"Scintillating conversation," Atlas replied.

"Yeah. Thrilling one-word answers."

"Yeah, well chill, Bro. Haven't gotten the manifesto yet."

Rex turned to Atlas. He couldn't resist the jab.

"Cute. What? A month? I think you like being seduced."

. . .

The next day, bracketed by roadside redwoods, two CHP vehi-cles, with headlights silently cycling, sat parked at obtuse angles across a country highway and created a single entrance lane. An unmarked dark vehicle glided through.

In front of Rex's and Gia's house, a black jacketed agent with FBI logo unlocked the taped front door for the most special of investigators, George Grimes, age 40, "young, gifted and black, moving on up" without the charm of a Jefferson. Out of respect, the jacketed agent addressed him, "Agent Grimes."

Grimes nodded, said nothing, and entered; the agent followed him.

In the dining room, Grimes stood in the middle; Grimes' eyes moved with the precision of a coordinated, robotic periscope. He silently scanned. The jacketed agent remained at the threshold.

Grimes viewed in sequence; a bra under the table, the wine-stained tablecloth, and photo of Wong. But he focused upon, picked up, and pondered the photo of Rex and his Seal team.

• • •

It was a bustling spring day, bright, cheery, and sunny; the kind of day that avid fans dream of, especially on opening day at Oracle Park.

The crowd was packed, the seat "top drawer." Overwhelming anticipation preceded the first pitch of the Diamondback Ace. His wind-up was followed by an almost simultaneous crack of the bat. Cheers rose with the crowd as the ball sailed over the center field fence.

But a buzz gave way to a vibration from Jansen's phone and a certain disappointment.

The screen revealed the text:

"Grimes wants you there."

• • •

Jansen was about 25 with white hair and green eyes, as meticulous and as clean cut as you could possibly imagine; black pants, white shirt, the kind of guy who might knock on a stranger's front door to inform that a rear tire looked low. That was the impression of all his co-workers at the data center of the San Francisco FBI facility.

His proficiency at culling disparate strands into actionable information had garnered the praise of his superiors, especially Grimes, willing to ride any horse to the top.

Grimes was sitting at his desk, searching the profile of Rex on the national physician data base when he heard the knock.

"Come in."

Jansen entered.

"Agent Grimes, something's going on. Activity on the Chinese circuit."

"Great. Put it in the briefing," Grimes replied. "I want to know everything there is to know about this."

Grimes handed Jansen the Seal Team photo.

• • •

In the log cabin big room, Gap sat before a large screen TV monitor. Rex walked in from the outside, refreshed from a night's sleep. Atlas emerged from the stairs to the basement.

"Going up the side. Want to join us?" Atlas shouted.

Gap pointed up at the screen.

"Should see this!"

The TV screen revealed a middle-aged reporter with a huge red bow tie, followed by side-by-side head shots of Govinda and Stern.

The reporter continued, "Nobel contender, Professor Harold Govinda, was found knifed to death on the northern coast. And in a nearby vehicle, global investor Tom Stern also was also murdered by a gunshot wound."

Atlas smiled and noted, "That son of a bitch's O.P.S., right?"

The reporter went on, "Both were found near the house of this man."

The TV revealed a head shot of Rex in a naval dress uniform.

"Doctor Rex Lee, a naval physician, the protege of Govinda, and the featured but absent speaker at yesterday's annual shareholders meeting of the Genometrics Corporation."

The TV then revealed a head shot of Gia.

"Doctor Lee and his wife, Gia Marina Lee, an astrobiologist, are missing and sought for questioning."

Atlas exclaimed, "This shit's getting real!"

. . .

In Zion National Park, Rex and Atlas meandered up a steep mountain trail of narrow breaks between boulders and trees with unexpected competitive zeal. Rex fell a little behind.

Rex yelled, "Hold up, Old Man. You owe me."

Atlas stopped. Rex used the opportunity to rush by him. Atlas voiced, "Oh yeah?"

Rex replied, "Saved your ass, didn't I?"

Now behind, Atlas pulled up his shirt, downed his pants, revealed a gunshot wound, and slapped his left buttocks.

"Still got a little left ass left."

Both rested. Atlas asked for specific clarity in his unique general way.

"End of the world shit I get. Brother, just break it down."

"This is about my future with Gia, America, your service in the military, and all you hold dear and queer. And, oh yes, the world could end because people could end."

"Yo, Dude. Gonna need more."

"How about 'The Killer'?" Rex had thought it through.

"Sure. If you pay him enough."

Rex nodded; the two resumed climbing.

"This has to go right, or nothing will matter. But if so, I'll have Mad Nobel Money."

"No need. The 'Killer' takes credit. For everything!"

They reached the summit.

"Credit? Got the card?" Rex asked.

Atlas pulled out a black card and held it up to Rex's face. Rex was both glad and incredulous. "Still active?"

"Latest Beau Coup model. Product of the perfect Soviet style hack. The 'Farm' can't shut it down until they figure it out."

They looked out at the vast yellow, white, red, orange stripped gorges and canyons of Zion.

Rex pumped his fist and exclaimed. "Okay then. Let's gitty up."

• • •

Below a sparsely clouded moon lit sky, a propeller driven cargo plane weaved over treetops as the river's edge sliced the curve of forested hills. The plane ascended to "jump" height.

Helmeted in camouflage fatigues, Rex and Atlas sat together while Gap, close by, slumped in slumber. Across from them, wide-eyed, awake was Keiko, "The Killer," an extremely composed Japanese man, age 35, well beyond meticulous, a seeker of perfection, one gory step at a time. With an oversized duffel bag at his feet, Keiko cleaned to a spit shine every component of his sniper rifle.

A jolt in the ride disturbed Gap. Rex, as jocular as Gap was stoic, mouthed off.

"Gap, welcome back! Heard you're from Brooklyn."

Gap, now feigning annoyance, replied, "Born Brooklyn. Raised Chicago. The hood!"

Rex was impressed, "White boy like you? How'd you get Gap?"

Gap finally smiled and genuinely laughed inside to himself. "Geoffrey Avery Parkinson the Fourth."

"No shit!?" Rex exclaimed.

Gap nodded, closed his eyes, and dosed off again. Rex looked at Atlas. Atlas smiled and shook his head.

Atlas got up, walked over, and sat next to Keiko. He stretched his neck to peer into Keiko's bag and saw a sheathed, ceremonial samurai short sword, a tanto.

Atlas bent down and then looked up into Keiko's face.

"What you got?" Atlas moved his hand toward the bag.

Keiko pulled the bag shut. He responded, politely but firmly.

"Please don't touch that."

A red light silently flashed.

Since he knew more about everyone than anyone, Atlas took charge.

"All right, ladies. Let's dance."

Keiko reassembled his rifle like a Rubic's Cube Champion.

Over the nocturnal airspace of the western Amazonian River basin, four men, in sequence, launched from the cargo doors.

THE UNSEEN WORLD

CHAPTER 13

THE HEEL OF THE
TRAFFICANTES

"...a frenzy for the gold."

Even though the worn wooden boat steamed steadily forward, the air was thick... so heavy on the tongue one could taste salt and the pungent decay of human remains, floating on the river every other mile. It was a distinctive smell, one well known to battlefield responders. As he stood at the bow alone, the intermittent smell compounded Rex's apprehension of what they might find up this unsearched branch of the Rio Solimo.

Perhaps, loneliness also amplified his awareness.

Keiko was in the cabin steering the craft, impassive, absorbed in more of a mood than a thought, wholly personal to himself. Their prior interaction was confined to a volunteer rescue of Taiwanese Buddhist medical personnel in Myanmar, hostages of a rogue paramilitary unit. There Rex witnessed in Keiko a total disregard for personal safety, only expected in those self-convinced to be invincibly invulnerable.

Always attentive in any setting, Keiko rarely expressed his opinion or emotion; but when he did, his insights were so often so infused with satiric irony, those present would find themselves laughing or, at least, smiling days later.

Atlas and Gap were at the stern. Whatever smell they might have smelt did not bother them. They ate and drank the last provisions of beer and most of the soul food of their choosing, all hurriedly mustered for the journey.

They were entwined in their own momentary pre-adolescent frivolity, like renegade cub scouts around a campfire telling sordid jokes, only understandable through their intimate familiarity. The days of "Don't ask; don't tell" were well behind them.

Their escapism made sense in one sense. Atlas, previously a contracted mercenary, had seen it all in special ops campaigns, well past enough to relish fully the rejuvenating power of diversion.

But Gap? That was another story. To Rex, he was a blank slate.

Rex removed from his pocket a plastic laminated head shot of Gia. He focused on her dark curly hair and reminisced how its soft waves would flow over his shoulders when she sat on his lap in a frontal embrace. He missed her far beyond measure. Now for the first time, he regretted his reluctance to start a family and embrace beyond their vows a new singularity.

Rex felt a tap on his shoulder and turned to see Gap, wide-eyed and smiling. Gap reached for the picture then held it out in front of them. He volunteered the obvious.

"Hot!" he said admiringly. Rex hesitated but took it as a compliment.

Gap continued to nod approvingly as he carried some fried chicken into the cabin for Keiko. Keiko bowed humbly and gratefully accepted it, even though it was not Japanese fried chicken.

A snapping sound…the boat's bow shuttered. Rex looked down upon the remnants of a leafless branch as it passed and scratched the side and bottom.

He looked up. In the distance, a single bark canoe floated slowly down from up stream. As it approached, Rex could make out a solitary elder native man sitting motionless, holding a laced-together bamboo oar. Approaching closer, the man was pale, emaciated, and seemingly too weak to row.

A thoroughly worn elder woman sat well behind the man. She held in her hands the head of a closed-eyed recumbent, naked gender indistinct child. Rex wondered if the woman had noticed that the child was not breathing.

As the boat passed, the woman turned and looked at Rex with a stare that penetrated through him. She then closed her eyes and bent forward in silent, tearful resignation.

Before Rex could hail the others to turn the boat around, a flotilla of canoes with saddened, sickened, suffering people passed them.

• • •

After passing the flotilla, the number of random canoes carrying wayward people fell off. For several hours the comrades had encountered no new souls traversing the river. While they had previously decided to set their overnight camp on an embankment, just as the sun was fully setting, they reached an unmarked village, littered around the edges of a natural river cul-de-sac.

At the center of the town, arranged on a horseshoe, sat a

miniature twin tower "Notre Dame." At one time stylish, but now a dilapidated colonial church, it was a prior tribute to the vast sums of Catholic monies that flowed freely out of gold-enriched Manaus in the 19th century.

The town was a half-circular patchwork of poorly kept, one story wooden dwellings of fading mix matched colors. The town was silent. The town was dark. The town was "dead."

Keiko and Gap were unloading nocturnal provisions, when Rex, standing in the town center next to Atlas, noticed a torch-light blossoming from the otherwise darkened church. As the torch approached, Rex could define the outline of a Franciscan robed priest. It was still hot and muggy. The robe had to have been donned quickly.

Father Bernardo was short, bald, and benign, and as he approached, a man of focused urgency.

"Señor, Señor!" the priest exclaimed.

• • •

Remaining silent, Bernardo urged Rex and Atlas to follow. He waved to the heads of villagers peering around the church's wall. Sparks of light gradually illuminated the dark interior. When Rex and Atlas entered, the church was well lit by multiple candles on the altar, and torches that buttressed from the wall.

The sight of human desolation was overwhelming.

The church was converted into a makeshift hospital. Sick natives of every age laid strewn supine on pews. Those who had expired were sequestered below, awaiting daylight to permit their removal. Only the altar was devoid of "patients."

Rex sat down next to a prostrated pale native girl. Though weak, she managed to flash a smile when Rex felt her radial pulse. He was grateful to find her without fever and with a pulse that was relatively strong. He detached Atlas' canteen and handed it to a native woman.

Suddenly, a pre-teen boy standing under a torch, collapsed. Atlas scooped him up and carried him to a vacant pew. Rex quickly examined the child, noticing the bulging veins of his neck and the declining strength of his pulse.

"Meu Deus!" Rex yelled to Atlas. "At, get my bag."

Atlas ran out and returned. Rex pulled out a stethoscope and listened to the boy's heart and lungs. Groggy at first, the boy blacked out.

Rex exclaimed, "My God! I hope I'm right."

He motioned to Atlas and the priest. "Set him higher."

The priest did not know what to do. Atlas placed his knee behind the back of the boy and with his hands under the boy's shoulders, raised him to 45 degrees.

Rex freed up a long sterile needle, and with gloved hands attached it to intravenous tubing linked to a large plastic syringe. Sensing what he should do, Atlas poured iodine on the boy's chest. Rex felt for the bottom of the child's breast plate between the chest and abdomen. He guided the needle through a space between the adjoining ribs and pulled back suction on the syringe aiming for the child's left shoulder.

"Come on! Come on!"

A wet tear rolled down Rex's cheek.

Suddenly, straw colored fluid, not blood, popped into the syringe. Rex pulled the plunger. The syringe filled rapidly. Immediately, the breathless child started breathing.

Rex pulled out fluid, detached the syringe, ejected the waste on to the wooden floor, reattached the syringe, and repeated the cycle over and over again, until no additional fluid could be expressed. The boy, though weak, flashed the broadest smile of Rex's career.

The priest was effusive, flashed his palms heavenward, and recited a latin liturgy he had not uttered since seminary.

After Rex had removed the needle and placed a bandage over the puncture site, Atlas gave Rex a hearty slap on the back.

"What in the name of Saint Francis of Assisi was that?"

"Tamponade," Rex replied. "Inflammatory fluid surrounding and crushing the heart."

"Damnation!" Atlas exclaimed. He walked away shaking his head, unable to wait to tell the others.

The inquisitive priest remained nearby and anxiously chattered on, hoping for a hopeful response, expecting that Rex might know something.

"Every day, more and more, they come. Cross the border, Señor. Guerrilla against trafficante."

Rex shook his head. "What about the authorities? Evacuation?"

"No law here, Señor," the priest explained.

Cut off. No one coming to help us. You men…a miracle. Wondering how you get here."

The magnitude of the situation was just beginning to dawn .on Rex.

"The region's aflame," Bernardo explained. "Whipped into a

fever, a frenzy for the gold."

"The gold?" Rex replied.

Exasperated, the priest continued.

"Sim Señor, Portuguese gold, O Caldeiro, 'The Cauldron.' Legend from Macau; Stolen from China… brought to Brasil by pirates. Colonial slavers in colonial times. Never believed true. No matter. They believe it!"

• • •

Some villagers had taken their own initiative to escape. Among those who could not, it took a day to gather the sick and the viable. By boat, the comrades transported them to a village far enough away from the chaos, but close enough to signal for provincial aid.

With much reluctance, Bernardo agreed to no burial for the "too soon" dead but assented to a ceremony of priestly prayers. Outside the church, the comrades assembled the bodies of his silenced choir, and solemnly placed them over a pagan pyre, and with torches ablaze, consumed them in a raging fire.

The day was exhausting; but the night's work had to be done.

• • •

In the boat's cabin, each man found what space they could to clean and render reliable their weaponry. The tense crowding amplified their muffled silence.

Finally, Atlas raised from his rifle and took charge. He looked around and seeing no initiative, turned to Rex.

"Okay. No one else is going to say shit. Time to come clean, Bro."

Gap and Keiko stopped abruptly what they were doing.

Atlas continued.

"Saving the species from a "f"ed up biological weapon... totally get it. Dropping into famine, pestilence, and a war zone of heavily armed drugged out guerrillas searching for some mythical Chinese gold? Man, that's one smelly fart! This shit is worse than Sudan."

Rex focused on Atlas. "Saved your life once."

Then he turned to Keiko. "And I would have saved yours, if you weren't so Bad Ass."

Rex looked at all of them.

"Not good enough? Okay. All I can tell you now is that it is all related. You all are going to have to trust me.

Think about it. Essentially, we are now on a medical mission. We four are the only medicine these people are going to get."

They looked around at each other and grudgingly nodded.

"Okay. We leave before dawn, so nobody sees us."

Rex walked out of the cabin. Outside, he took the amulet necklace out of his pocket and re-examined it.

CHAPTER 14

JOIA

The mission had been organized at light warp speed. From high Utah to deep Amazon in mere days. But already they were in the "shit."

Rex took the point, never an expectation for a "jungle doc." But he had the knowledge and the perspective of what they might be up against. Even more importantly, he had their respect.

It was Rex, followed by Keiko, next Gap, and last Atlas with his watchful eye on the priest, whose experience of the locale exceeded the utility of their topographical maps. Although he had lived in the region for decades, only one other time had the priest ventured northward in the current direction.

Earlier in his posting, Bernardo had promised his mentor, Bishop Francisco da Silva, that every fifth year, he would perform a monastic "walkabout" of varying duration to reinforce his connection to nature. Twice westward, he had traversed up the river in a small canoe and then embarked to go either north or south.

Among the villagers, there had been random rumors of criminal brutality, forcing indigenous peoples into hasty and uncharted migrations. But well over a month had passed. He had seen no objective evidence.

As he had explained earlier to Rex, he, Bernardo, may have been the only outside person ever to have had contact with an "Unseen"... that is until the recent treachery of the trafficantes. It was during a frenzy of their violence that his "Jewel" was lost from her tribe, and then swept away by a torrential downpour that flash flooded an otherwise dry tributary.

It was a miracle that he had found her, and even more of a miracle that she rallied back to life.

Unfamiliar with northern surroundings, Bernardo had decided to venture not far. His initial direction was reassured by the position of the sun. However, after no more than 10 kilometers, the pointer of his compass had flipped wrongly several times. But it had taken time to detect and confirm.

Spooked by this finding, Bernardo decided to turn back, guessing as best he could. Distracted by the compass, he slipped and tumbled 20 meters through a crevice of brush and trees. He blacked out after hitting his head against a tree and later awoke, confused with no sun to guide him. He followed the path of least resistance downward, first slowly, and then rapidly like a rain droplet on tilted glass.

At the bottom, he suddenly encountered her outstretched supine body, immobile and exposed, barely hovering above death. Although her face was curiously radiant, her body was very cold and unconscious.

At that point, he did the only thing he could physically do. He gathered her body and carried her downward over the evaporating water of an otherwise dry channel bed, reasoning that eventually through gravity, all water magically merges together.

Somehow, he reached the Solimo, but was too tired to carry her further. So, he placed her body in the river, grasped her across her chest, and guided her floating body, while struggling against the river's tide to maintain contact with the shore.

When he reached the village, a plethora of inhabitants carried her to the church. They laid her on a pew. Bernardo did not deter them. The indigenous words they uttered had no meaning to him. Before he could initiate a traditional Catholic prayer, she had displayed signs of improving, warming from fingers and toes to her chest. By morning, before he awoke, she had already arisen to thank him.

She was a physically robust girl of thirteen, a head taller than village girls of the same age. Agile and strong, but most impressively she was absorbingly intelligent, especially facile in language. Within weeks she could speak conversational Portuguese. Although he had not heard, much less spoken English in many years, he dusted off his books, and together they studied.

And then suddenly, it was as if the sky departed from the earth, removing justice, hope, and any degree of civility.

Although a few injured natives had floated down the river, his village had little, if any time to escape before the trafficantes arrived. They descended, slaughtered the infirm, rounded up pubescent and pre-pubescent girls, and brought to the villagers scourges from which they had no immunity. Then nonchalantly as they arrived, they left. Having reasoned that access to the river could be useful, they encamped less than 20 kilometers away. They feared no retribution and left the remaining to die.

Now, Rex and the comrades were coming for them.

CHAPTER 15

PAYBACK

After leaving the village, the camouflaged comrades macheted a path through the thick overgrowth of jungle brush. Now they were ascending through the rainforest piedmont of far western Brazil, the hilly region before the Andes, the Amazon River's most distant source.

Though he tended to fall behind, the priest was flushed with an adrenaline rush. He was determined to get "His Jewel" back.

Blending into their surroundings, walking deliberately with their rifles pointed down, the comrades halted when Rex raised his right fist. They stopped, dropped for cover, and pulled the priest down.

Something ahead in the trees over a ridge.

Rex took out his binoculars. Through it, he saw taut ropes hanging from a tree, suspending inert weight below.

On Rex's signal, they rose partially and crouching, moved forward.

They reached a small grassy clearing before a tree-filled ridge. Above them dangled three lynched native men with penetrating wounds and necks grotesquely stretched on knotted rope.

To a man, each comrade thought to himself... No trespassing!

Must be getting close.

Rex moved forward cautiously to examine as Gap pushed past Keiko and tugged on Rex's shoulder. Gap placed the barrel of his rifle across Rex's chest and nudged Rex backwards. Rex then grabbed a large rock and tossed it into the clearing.

WHOOSH.

The floor of the clearing gave way. All peered over the side to blades pointing upward.

"I guess he did learn something in 'The Sa..tan,'" Atlas remarked.

Rex smiled at Gap.

"Thanks, Bro."

Gap flexed Rex a thumbs up.

After winter, flowers explode from fruit trees. But it takes time for carrots to grow.

Now was time to plant!

• • •

The camp laid below lush hills. A watch tower stood atop the tallest. Its guards chatted rather than peer out over their machine gun mounts.

Below, no tents. Just makeshift bamboo barracks in parallel rows. Parked armored vehicles stood at a single-lane dirt road entrance expanded from a trail. Trafficantes milled around a common square, laughed, gambled, drank, ate, "dissed" one another, and in one instance, squared off to fight.

This was an army with serious down time.

From a hill above, the four comrades and the priest huddled.

Crunching footsteps approached them. Keiko instantly leapt out, wrenched the neck of a patrolling bandit, and dragged the body into the brush.

Keiko shrugged to the priest, "Sorry, Padre."

Rex took charge.

"Atlas, set up just a little further down. Gap, get to the tower. Keiko, roam the periphery. Attack at maximum leverage. Padre, you stick with me."

It took a harrowing 15 minutes for Atlas to sneak undetected around and above the camp's floral covering.

At the knoll, Atlas set up machine guns, mortars, and a silencer-mounted sniper rifle on a tripod.

Gap climbed the tower on its shielded side. Reaching the top, he stabbed one guard and threw a knife into the chest of the other, then knelt below the gun mounts.

On an opposite hill, two trafficantes sat, smoking weed behind a barracks. Keiko removed a knife from the third in their patrol. He stood up from his camouflaged position and fired two muffled shots into the heads of the two stoned trafficantes.

Commandante Ignacio Solis, in sharp appointed fatigues, holstered a SAT phone as he exited from a small building and entered the central clearing. He motioned to the trafficantes to assemble.

Troop carriers approached. At the head was Cubano, a tall, slender, white bearded man. He wore thick wire dark glasses, light tan fatigues and a round cap... a Vegas double for Fidel.

Cubano exited and saluted the Commandante.

"Oh shit!" Atlas uttered as he looked across the forest to Rex.

Commandante motioned to two men. They entered another building and brought out a group of fifty twenty native girls. The trafficantes taunted them as they lined up in the center.

Commandante examined each girl. He paused in front of a 13 year old. It was Joia, much taller and more striking than the others. He turned her head and looked behind her left ear. He waved to two trafficantes.

Joia spat in his face. The men dragged her into a bamboo shack. Others removed the remaining girls into a shelter. Bernardo pulled on Rex.

"Señor, that's her, My Jewel. She is still alive!"

Rex cautioned him.

"Padre, remain here."

Rex stole his way down through the brush and approached the shack.

SPLAT.

A dead trafficante with knife in hand fell short of Rex's feet.

Rex looked up. Atlas looked through his sniper scope and flashed a thumbs up. Rex nodded and then peered through an open window.

Inside, the two men had bound Joia face down across a table. Rex leaped through the window and knocked both men unconscious with the butt of his pistol. But the pistol discharged.

BANG!

Outside, the camp startled. Frozen trafficantes stared at Commandante. Unhappy at the prospect of losing his prize, he signaled a platoon to enter.

No need to hang back now!

Atlas dropped a projectile into the mortar casing.

SWOOSH. BOOM. The body parts of 8 men flew.

Gap stood defiantly, fired from the tower, and pried open Hell.

RATATATATATATATATAT.

Trafficantes scrambled for cover and returned automatic fire to the tower and the knoll.

SWOOSH. RATATATATATATATAT. BOOM! Chaos! Body parts everywhere.

Behind the building, Rex pushed Joia and then himself out of the window.

From the periphery, Keiko "lit up" armored vehicles with RPGs.

BOOM! BOOM! BOOM!

The priest made his way into the girls' shelter. Eyes of terror were followed by tears of hope.

Keiko ran through the camp, stabbed startled trafficantes, dodged bullets, then leaped over and behind a vehicle.

RATATATATATATATATAT!

Concentrated automatic fire whittled away at the vehicle.

Lying on his back, Keiko pulled a pin and tossed a grenade blindly high over the firing vehicles.

The grenade fell into an ammunition cluster.

BOOM...BOOM, BOOM...BOOM...BOOM!

Body parts everywhere!

• • •

At the top of the hill, the priest herded the girls into the rainforest. A column of trafficantes reorganized by Commandante, assembled behind personnel carriers.

Keiko signaled the direction to retreat.

"Rex!" Keiko called out.

Rex and Joia tried that direction, but return fire was "too hot."

Atlas and Gap continued to rain down fire. Bullets, RPGs, and mortars, whizzed from multiple directions, blowing apart windows, chairs, doors, and vehicles, propelling shards of angled glass.

Joia pointed the way. Rex and Joia ran to the rainforest in the opposite direction from Keiko.

Gap descended the tower as Atlas unleashed heavy automatic fire from two machine gun pods.

In the rainforest clearing, some of the girls became hysterical, and others froze upon seeing three hanged uncles. The priest calmed them as best he could; then led them carefully around.

The girls and priest now awaited ahead. Keiko and Gap leaped over camouflaging bushes and ran past a kneeling Atlas.

When the trafficantes approached, Atlas pushed a lever and "cancelled" the clearing forever.

BOOM! BOOM! BOOM!

The IED traps blew the column apart.

• • •

Rex and Joia rushed out of a clearing toward a waterfall.

In the distance, trafficantes pursued.

Rex and Joia rushed up a hill of thinning trees.

Trafficantes ran over uneven plain and jumped like jack rabbits over tuffs of tall grass.

Although it was now easier and more accurate to shoot, Commandante issued his command.

"Nao atire!"

At the edge of the waterfall, Joia pointed downward at the rocky borders adjoining the river below. Joia guided Rex. They descended and reached a quarter of the way down.

As rolling thunder crashed over the waterfall, Joia led Rex to a narrow ledge extending from rocky boulders into and under torrents of liquid death.

She slid, foot to foot, facing the boulders, and vanished into mist.

Rex followed as the trafficantes and Commandante reached the rocky perch above them.

A trafficante raised his rifle and fired.

"Nao!" the Commandante exclaimed in a fit of anger.

The bullet struck below Rex's searching foot and shattered supporting rock. It gave way, and Rex plummeted through tumultuous water into raging river. Floating into the distance, he sank below line of sight.

The Commandante slapped the disobedient man. He waved his right index finger from chin to chin. Trafficantes then tossed the stricken man out over the boulders and watched him crunch on jagged rock.

• • •

Atlas was the last comrade to reach the moored boat. He look a long back. But finally, he jumped on board as the boat puttered away.

• • •

At dusk, near the river's rocky edge, Rex's unconscious body floated face up until his left ankle snagged a boulder cleft. His torso undulated in the river current from side to side, until his head struck a boulder, and his foot released. As he sank, bubbles popped on the river surface.

• • •

Now dark, except for faint moonlight, eyes from above looked through the water to the wavering outline of a shimmering figure.

Joia knelt over Rex's submerged body at the river's edge. She cupped her hand around his neck and lifted Rex's head out of the water. His fixed blank eyes stared.

She cupped her mouth around his and blew into his body.

She released him. Rex's head drifted below the surface. A nose appeared. His face rose out of the water; eyes closed.

Unconscious, Rex coughed up cold, stilled water.

CHAPTER 16

COMMITTING
TO THE MASTER

"Are you a King?"

In the healing hut, a flickering flame illuminated Rex's unconscious body. His naked heavily bruised torso laid on a wooden slab.

Amu, a very old yet vibrant man, reached into a large woven basket and removed an antique Portuguese mirror.

Zo, his son, a native man of 60 years but with a face and body of 35, reached out and restrained Amu's shoulder.

Their dialogue was conducted in their native indigenous tongue.

"Father, you must reconsider," Zo urged.

Amu scoffed and shook his head.

"Father, I beg you. Do not utter the healing words."

Amu looked at Joia. She sat outside 25 feet away, around a fire pit. Seeing Amu's gaze, she rose and walked into the hut.

Zo would not relent.

"Father, alone, his spirit did not come. Others will follow. Let nature take him."

"Did he let nature take her?"

Amu pointed to Joia.

Amu covered Rex with an animal hide and sat down. Joia sat on the other side close to Rex's ear and translated Amu's words into English.

"Rex, we bless you for the return of our Joia. Cold waters have stilled your body. But there is a rhythm deep inside you."

Amu tapped softly and repeatedly on the wooden slab. One, two, three…one, two, three.

"Can you hear this rhythm? You may wish to tell us, or you may not. It does not matter.

"Because the rhythm causes a light to emerge, to glow in the center of your body…this body."

Amu reached for a torch and held it out over the center of Rex's body.

"You may even feel the heat of this light. You may see the light from the inside. You may even begin to feel the rhythm."

One, two, three…one, two, three.

Amu tapped on Rex's chest over his sternum.

"The rhythm, the warmth, the light, and the fire, all speak to the perfection inside you."

Amu nodded to Joia.

Now above the torch, Joia held the mirror out over Rex's body.

"The light, the rhythm, and the heat sink deep, deep, deep inside you."

Amu again nodded to Joia.

Joia took away the mirror. Amu stopped tapping and removed the torch.

"Now, I command you…to take a deep breath."

Rex started to breathe. Rex took in a very, very, very deep breath.

"And as you breathe out, this power… these feelings… these thoughts, sink deep, deep, deep inside you. In daylight, you will awake to the light of a new self."

Rex breathed out. Joia and Amu exited the hut.

Breathing calmly with eyes closed, Rex laid alone.

• • •

Later, in the corner of an adjoining hut, Amu snored deeply. Joia, sleeping across the one large room, suddenly opened her eyes and sat up.

Minutes later, Zo, stealthily wound his way around the outside of the village. He approached the healing hut and peered inside. Through dimly transmitted light, he saw the outline of Rex's supine body on the slab.

As he entered the hut, Zo saw Joia with eyes closed sitting at Rex's head. Quietly, Zo retreated.

• • •

Flickering ruby red was all he could see; the gurgling of a creek and the chatter of lusting birds all he could hear, until self-awareness returned. Then slowly, Rex opened his eyes wide. Above, on fluttering branches were his clothes, swaying just enough to allow sun rays through.

Laying on and covered by woven cloth, Rex sat up at the edge of a hillside creek. He grimaced and held both forearms. Below through the rainforest, indistinct human figures milled around.

He descended fully clothed and entered the village. Villagers were not seemingly impressed by his presence; children ran; adults performed their chores. Finally, a sitting old woman flashed a smile, and some teenage girls giggled.

Everyone exhibited strong upright posture, glowing olive skin devoid of wrinkles, supple musculature, and perfect proportions. Absence of discord. Total Beauty!

As if on cue, all acknowledged him except for Zo. Across the center, Zo glared at him before entering Amu's hut. A smiling Joia emerged from the hut and walked to Rex.

"Oi, Señor Rex. Como vai?" she asked.

"Como se diz em Portuguese? Muito 'sore,'" he replied.

"A minha esposa e brasileira. Falo portuguese um pouco. Quero falar ingles; e possivel?" ("My wife is Brazilian. I speak a little Portuguese. I wish to speak English; it is possible?")

"Muito bom, Señor Rex. Are you really a King?" she asked.

"No, no." Rex shook his head and laughed. "Where are we?"

"Your people call us 'The Unseen.' I am the only one seen beyond here. 'Nardo' taught me your language. I teach my brother everything."

Rex looked around. The entire tribe smiled at him.

"Would you like to meet The Master?"

"Very much so," Rex replied.

As she turned, under her left ear on the margin of her neck, Rex saw "JING," the Chinese hexagram for "The Well."

As Rex and Joia entered the hut, Zo stood in front of a sitting Amu and held out an arrow. Amu, unmoved, looked toward Rex and Joia.

Zo broke the arrow and tossed it down. He turned in front of Rex, eyeball to eyeball, and brushed Rex aside as he left.

"Señor Rex, a man of 700 moons should have better manners," Amu uttered as smiling Joia translated.

Amu beckoned Rex to sit beside him as Joia continued.

"The Master wants to know who is the man who returns his lost daughter. What is your work?"

"Doctor," stated Rex.

Amu smiled and held up his hands to heaven.

"A great honor. You come on the day of 100 moons that our doctors perform the Great Healing!"

• • •

Amu, in ceremonial garb, sat with eyes closed in the middle of a central clearing. Twelve empty backless stools surrounded him. The villagers formed a circle. Eager to know the sequence, Rex asked Joia, "Where are the doctors?"

"We wait," she volunteered.

Amu rose and opened his eyes.

"The doctors are arriving," Joia explained.

Amu walked around the human circle and examined individuals face to face. He stopped in front of an elderly female. He held a pouch over her. She moved to sit on a stool.

Amu chose 10 additional people of all ages. Just one stool left.

Amu stopped in front of Zo. Zo stared across Amu to Rex. Amu noted the stare and shook his head. Amu smiled at Rex but moved on. He stopped at Joia and chose her.

All the "doctors" rose and held hands. Amu chanted briefly. Zo looked despondent. Then, the circle dispersed.

• • •

It was a long night for Rex, one in which he barely slept. Alone in a hut, Rex laid on his back with a woven cloth covering him.

• • •

The next day, Amu was meditating alone when Joia and Rex, now clothed as an Unseen, entered his hut.

"Amu, Señor Rex has a request," Joia revealed.

Not needing a translation, Amu replied, "Let him say it in his own words."

"I am a doctor, but I want to be a healer."

Amu examined both of Rex's hands.

"Understandable. Having been healed, you wish to heal. But you are already a healer. You want to be a Master, is it not so?"

At first slow to respond, Rex replied emphatically, "Yes!"

Amu was delighted, "Good! We start now."

CHAPTER 17

THE QUANTUM TRUTH
OF A MADMAN

"One is the Only Number."

With the zeal of a Hercules anointed, Rex set upon the tasks Amu appointed. Others might have demanded different tasks. But for Amu, there would be three. Unlike the skills Wong imparted focused on speed, agility, co-ordination, and anticipation, Amu's would focus on strength, both physical and mental. It had been just one day when Rex was a breath away from death.

Steep rainforest hills stood before him. Rex encircled his arm pits and shoulders around two heavily thickened woven ropes that together forced him to bear an additional quarter of his weight. Then through thick vegetation and over uneven rock, Rex followed the steep ascent of Amu and Joia along a mountain creek. He bore the weight without extending arms and hands to balance on branches and boulders.

They reached an intersection of creek that held a massive boulder. Over and around water jetted and flowed.

While Amu and Joia observed, Rex sat under the rock. His arms were attached to ropes lashed to the trunks of two trees

R. Chapman Wesley

juxtaposed across the creek from each other. Amu beckoned Rex to rise. As Rex held tight, continuous waves of torrential water pounded his back and contorted his face from the strain. Finally, when his legs turned into gelatin, Amu relented.

• • •

Later that night by the light of two torches, Amu and Joia huddled for warmth under a woven blanket while Rex sat with his back to them at the edge of the creek. Two factions of ants, one red, the other black, scurried in waves over the front and back of his upper torso, biting with their jaws and needling his skin with their horns. Rex grimaced and battled the pain with muted utterances.

Joia translated Amu's words.

"If you ignore them, they will tire of biting you."

It took time for the unconscious war within his frontal lobes to subsist. But when the truce was finally made, through the subconscious mediation of his midbrain, calm enveloped Rex's face, and numbness welled up as an anesthetic moat around his body. Gradually the bugs grew disinterested with no adrenaline to extract. They stopped biting him, then discovered and attacked each other. Swirls of colorful legions on his skin compressed into nodes of insect blood. Enemy ants crawled over the depleted carcasses of exoskeletons to attack, but then succumbed, falling to the ground in micro-clumps of slaughter.

• • •

The next day, before first light of dawn, Amu's final test was to be Rex's alone. Or so he thought.

Loping like a nocturnal panther after prey, Zo cloaked himself in jungle green and followed Rex with bow slung over his shoulder and a satchel of arrows.

At dawn, Rex stood before a mountain of packed trees, jagged boulders, and narrow crevices. A rope around his waist was attached to a 2 by 3 ft solid log.

Just as in the day before, Rex's momentum was slowed by a carried weight. Anywhere along the way, Zo could easily have attacked, then hidden Rex's reviled body in a manner never found.

Now directly in front of Rex, Zo stood, no more than 20 feet away. Zo blended into floral leaves with his bow drawn down upon Rex's beating, blood engorged heart. Zo was an "Unseen." To Rex, he was invisible.

But silently, Zo released the tension and paused to stare at Rex, who was completely unaware. He then moved behind a tree. He would hold back for a more rewarding satisfaction; to witness Rex fail.

Initially, Rex ascended steadily but then struggled against a stack of snagging trees. As the space between trees narrowed, entrapment of the log increased, and with it, frustration and kernels of doubt. Then Rex resolved no matter what, he would reach the summit. It was simply going to take time… one step at a time.

Zo was impressed. Rex surpassed the tree line but then confronted even more treacherous barriers, overhanging boulders and loose rock. Going further would require not only sheer strength but also foresight to avoid the dead-end of a hidden vertical maze.

Rex had reached a split ledge with edges separated by ten feet across a 400-foot vertical drop. As Rex contemplated this obstacle, he concluded there was only one way to cross without detaching the rope.

Rex threw the log up to a crevice between boulders. The log lodged in the hole and grinded its edges against loose rock. Rex swung across the vertical drop. As he landed on the opposite ledge, the log dislodged and fell through the drop. The momentum of the swinging log nearly pulled him to his death. After straining against the pendulum, Rex stilled the rope and pulled up the log. It was a feat that Zo begrudgingly admired.

Finally, Rex pulled himself over a flat boulder at the summit. Exhausted, lying on his back, Rex saw an eagle soaring above him.

As he rolled over to rise, he saw an eagle feather protruding from a crevice in a nearby rock. He reached into the crevice and found a green jade Chinese box. It contained a miniature scroll of brittle paper with an ink infused message written in English that repeated as he unrolled it.

The brittle scroll lasted just long enough for Rex to read three iterations of a repeating singular message before it disintegrated in a light breeze:

"One is the only number. The only number is One. Wherever there is truth, there is The One. Wherever there is the absence of truth, there is the absence of One. Zero is not nothing. And Zero is not the absence of One. Zero is no thing! Zero is One, through thinking and revealing One, becoming One. One plus zero is One, was One, and will always be One. One is the only number."

How or when it had gotten there was uncertain. Was it the

repetitions in "quantum" truth of a madman? Did only the madman know it was placed there?... Waiting for him, specifically him???

In the chain of causation, perhaps it was not the madman's choice to choose. Perhaps, it was his vision to subsume a mission, and in that recognition, set in motion a journey.

CHAPTER 18

INITIATION

As Rex wound his way back to the village, he heard muted shouts and laughter as he approached a clearing carved out of dense rainforest.

Rex witnessed Zo and two other men spinning, leaping, and swinging at each other in the rhythmic dancing combat of capoeira.

Rex waved at them. They froze upon seeing him. He approached and displayed his eagle feather. One man looked at it, took it, and excitedly showed it to the other.

Smirking in superiority, Zo invited Rex into the center of the clearing. Rex, confident as never before, relished the challenge. From a bowlegged stance, Zo pivoted forward and swung his foot around. Anticipating the move, Rex arched his head backward, rendering the thrust harmless. Rex forced a smile; the aggression unnerved him. But now was not the time to back down.

Rex assumed Zo's stance and duplicated Zo's move.

The two backed away from each other, but then faced off again. Zo attacked in the opposite direction, punched into Rex's chest and sent Rex airborne. Zo stood over Rex, now thoroughly dazed.

"Voce nao pertence aqui. (You do not belong here.)" Zo

exclaimed in Portuguese and pointed in an outward direction.

"Saia agora antes que seja tarde demais! (Leave now before it is too late!)"

Zo walked away with raging eyes. The two men followed.

Later, as it grew dark, Rex sat in the clearing alone, still dazed, not from the punch and the resultant physical pain, but rather his alienation from the zealous opponent he desperately needed to win over.

Frogs began to ribbett. A droplet of rain splatted on Rex's shoulder. He rose and walked out of the clearing. A light wind swayed the tops of trees.

• • •

Bands of lightening, peals of thunder, and hordes of howling wind, impassioned the ribbetting of rain-crazed frogs. Raindrops condensed into wavy sheets so blinding and thick that up and down were momentarily indistinguishable.

Beyond, an accumulating flash flood churned through a cavernous gorge. A foot bridge with two hand ropes swayed wildly in gusting wind.

Zo and his companions at one end urged Joia and the old woman to cross. But terrified, they could not move. The men slowly advanced towards them.

A flash of lightning struck a tree above. The shockwave of the thunderclap added downward velocity to the shattered bark. It severed one hand rope, and mute, as if accepting her fate, the old woman fell to her death.

Joia clung to the remaining hand rope. Sudden gusts of wind were at times so strong, the loose hand rope was pushed to vertical.

The two men and Zo bridged themselves arm to arm on the remaining hand rope but could not reach Joia. From above, Rex rushed to join the men.

Rex crawled below them on the foot rope but lost leverage. His body fell off, but he maintained his grasp with one hand. Swinging his other hand up to the rope, his body dangling, he moved hand over hand toward Joia.

Rex pulled himself up, grabbed the remaining hand rope, and connected arm to arm to Zo. He extended his free arm to Joia. With her feet on the foot rope, Joia slid behind each man, back to back, and reached the foot bridge entrance. Each man then slid, hand to hand, foot to foot, off the bridge.

Exhausted, Zo smiled and nodded at Rex.

• • •

Now, deep night at the village of the "The Unseen," the corpse of the old woman laid on a wooden pile. Surrounding villagers sang a rhythmic but woeful dirge. With a torch, Amu lit the pyre. Flames consumed the old woman. Her sparks meandered upward.

Early the next day, villagers assembled in a circle. Amu carried from his hut a golden pot with Chinese calligraphy for "Ting," The Cauldron. He kneeled before the pyre, took a large wooden spoon, scooped up some ashes, and mixed them in the pot. Amu then disappeared into his hut to remain alone.

In the rainforest clearing later that day, Rex played out his own cycles of Qigong, Tai Chi, and Kung Fu with exceptional balance and flexibility, exceeding the skill of Wong.

To what Rex previously possessed, the rainforest bestowed upon him; the focus of the cobra; the lightness of a high tree monkey; the hearing of the dawn cave bat; the stretch of a climbing panther; the precision of the rainbow hummingbird; and the diving speed of a hawk at prey; all added to the strength of an unshakable will.

Zo and the two men entered the clearing and silently observed. They gestured at Rex's capability. When Rex finished, the three approached.

Zo motioned for Rex to follow him and to the others to remain behind.

• • •

In the rainforest near the waterfall, Rex held Zo's bow. Zo pointed to a hanging coconut. Rex drew an arrow on the bow and shot the coconut. Zo smiled and motioned Rex to follow.

At the edge of the waterfall, Zo stood at the precipice and tossed a coconut above raging waters. He grabbed the bow from Rex and fired an arrow into the falling coconut. Rex smiled.

Zo handed the bow to Rex and picked up another coconut. Zo tossed the coconut upward. Rex struck it at its apogee (high point).

Zo smiled and picked up another coconut. He flashed three fingers at Rex. Rex shook his head in momentary disbelief.

Zo tossed it. Rex struck the coconut three times; at its apogee, as it fell, and just above the river. Zo smiled broadly.

• • •

That evening in Amu's hut, Rex, Joia, Zo, and the two men sat at Amu's feet. Zo stood up in front of Rex. With Joia translating, Amu proclaimed.

"Zo has requested that you join 'The Unseen.' Do you accept?"

Rex stood and faced Zo.

"Yes."

Rex and Zo clasped their fists and hugged.

• • •

In the village of "The Unseen," in ceremonial dress, Rex sat at the edge of a fire upon which Amu sprinkled purple dust. The fire flared into dancing violet flames that projected an aromatic mist which tingled every fiber of Rex's nostrils. The mist expanded every cul-de-sac sac of Rex's lungs. Within the center of his head, it was as if his brain was split apart and then fused back together.

The cerebral expansion and contraction induced a level of relaxation Rex had never felt before.

The village encircled him. They pressed forward to see every sight, to hear each softly spoken word, to sense the new presence of a soul in rapture.

Amu held up a cup for all to see, then offered it to Rex.

Without hesitation, Rex drank the entire cup. His eyes rolled and focused upward as his lids closed down. His head drifted backwards.

With a wooden ladle from a brown clay cistern, Amu poured water upon Rex's forehead. Then Amu took a flaming torch from Zo, extended it over Rex's closed eyes as Joia and Amu whispered into his ears.

"Born from Water, now consumed by an Inner Mounting Flame!"

• • •

Rock shattered below Rex's foot before the shot echoed through his ears.

Rex fell backwards. Sheets of water smashed into his core like shrapnel, projecting him into a tumbling wave of liquid chaos which suffocated his throat and filled his lungs. He drowned in mid-air. Pancaking into the river removed the last vestige of conscious awareness.

His body was surrounded, yet weightless, floating, disembodied in a vast darkness. Only a subconscious remnant registered the slowing of his heart that waned into the finality of a cold stillness.

It was from this cold stillness, from a complete absence of bodily vibration, that the light emerged. At first, an oscillating blue shimmer reflecting on a liquid surface, it blossomed into a golden yellow that grew in intensity with enveloping warmth.

A small hand cupped around his neck and lifted his mouth out of the river to a Breath and from cold silence to the sudden sound of water trickling over uneven rocks.

After the soft hand released him, and he sunk below again, a schreaching eagle rose out of the river. It ascended and circled the waterfall, the village, the rainforest, and the mountain, then rose through feathery clouds toward the Sun as the Earth dissolved below.

Other eagles emerged from clouds, first a few, then by the thousands. All flying in cacophonous squealing toward an enlarging Sun.

The first eagle arrived. It crashed into the Sun and morphed into a dark figure seated below a branching tree. The figure blended into the Sun, which then contracted into a single point of light. The point of light then exploded into a silent Super Nova Flash.

• • •

Rex awoke, weak and stunned. Zo pulled Rex to his feet and hugged him.

Later that night in a hut to himself, Rex laid alone and stared at his clothes hanging above him. Sitting up, he pulled them down. The amulet and the photo of Gia were undisturbed within them.

• • •

The sun rose over The Amazon.

At dawn in the rainforest clearing, Zo instructed Rex in capoeira; now his equal in grace. The two rested under a tree.

Zo extended each finger of his right hand in sequence from pinky to index. He then forged the four fingers with his thumb into a well-held fist.

Zo turned to Rex and spoke in Portuguese.

"You and I are Brothers. None can change that. For many thousands of Moons, 'The Unseen' have said, 'One is the only number; One Mind, One Heart, One Body, One Soul; Four Angels woven into One.'"

The two were now linked, woven into a synchronistic connection reminiscent of the struggles of mindful men long gone.

Now the time was right. Rex took out a photo of Gia and showed it to Zo. Zo smiled.

Rex then took a stick and drew in the dirt the I Ching hexagram of *The Well*.

"O Poço"

Zo's surprised eyes gave way to a nod.

CHAPTER 19
"O POÇO"—*THE WELL*

Zo remained outside the hut when Rex entered wearing the amulet.

Noticeably not his jovial self, Amu motioned for Rex to sit down next to Joia. She translated.

"So, you seek *The Well*?"

"Yes, Master."

"Are you like the Portuguese 3,500 moons ago?"

Dumbfounded, Rex shook his head.

"You come to here thirsty, seeking *The Well*. Perhaps you should have been like the English pirate who found *The Well* and then became thirsty?"

Amu looked at Rex, expecting an answer, but Rex remained silent, having none.

"Untie the rope, break the jug, and bathe in the eternal source," Amu insisted.

"The waters of *The Well* you seek are no different from the healing leaf."

"But submerging my leaf into the waters of *The Well* can create the power of a thousand leaves." Rex replied.

Amu scoffed at him.

Amu took his index finger and repeatedly pointed it into Rex's chest.

"Not even the water of *The Well*… There is nothing more powerful than *The Well*… already inside you."

"But Master, I must return. The lives of many depend upon me."

"There is always the rise and fall of the many… One. Only One. There is only One for which to return. Take back what you already have. Lest others seek what you leave behind."

But sympathetic to his predicament, Amu begrudgingly relented.

"But you speak your truth. And for this, we grant to you … a gift."

Amu went to his trunk. He took out a green crystal and placed it into Rex's palm.

"Add this to your amulet. Your motives… are pure. But too many others, who have never seen us, are not."

Then Amu cupped Rex's left palm around Rex's left ear, and leaned forward, whispering as Joia whispered into Rex's right ear.

"Listen very, very carefully. Lest your seeking finds regret. The Grandmothers are saying, 'Climbing down often more dangerous than climbing up.'"

• • •

With the amulet around his neck, rope around his side, and an empty water pouch slung over his shoulder, Rex followed Zo.

Towards the afternoon sun they ran, matching step to step,

like conjoined locomotives, adroitly pulling the ultra-light weight of an invisible cargo. Their speed was only limited by the density of the forest and the scale of rocky hills.

Down the other side, they were wading across a waist-deep creek when just ahead they heard the rumbling of staccato words.

Ducking below water, they swam to the adjacent shore, then slithered through waist-high brush toward a stand of trees.

Away from Commandante's supervision, trafficantes on the opposite bank enjoyed a respite from their search for Rex, (an obviously dead gringo). They dedicated to the mission the degree of seriousness they secretly thought it deserved. They bathed, swam, snorted, and smoked more than just cigars.

But on the nearby bank, a resolute older trafficante stood just 40 feet ahead of Rex and Zo. He struck a match, lit a wide cigar, and gestured with his middle finger to the platoon. He was manning a relegated guard post and seemed none too happy about it.

Zo pointed left, but as he started to creep forward, he snapped a dry branch. CRACK! It startled the trafficante so much that he lost his grip and "cigar-singed" his palm. He called out. His platoon mates stood and stared. They gathered their weapons.

With weapon drawn the trafficante walked slowly but directly forward. Zo brandished his knife. But Rex shook his head. Now just five feet away, Rex, embroidered in leafy green and brush, rose directly in front of the trafficante next to the nearest tree. The trafficante abruptly stopped and recoiled, like a ghost-spooked cat. His eyes followed left and right, then over the tree, all the way to branches high above.

The soldiers across the way began to laugh and chide the

trafficante, telling him to consider giving up "cigars." He sighed, relented, turned around, and sat against the tree with his back right next to Zo and Rex.

Now with time short, Zo stood next to Rex and pointed upward, causing Rex to scowl in disbelief. But before Rex could sign his reluctance, Zo was already up. So, Rex followed him up the tree. Near the top, with cover from a rustling wind, they jumped and swung from branch to branch, accompanied by the chattering hoots of high tree monkeys.

• • •

It was a moon-filled early night. Because of the trafficantes' presence, they had been forced to take a circuitous route. Now finally, they had reached the waterfall, the point at which Rex would proceed alone, and Zo would return to the village.

With water crashing over boulders above, Rex and Zo shuffled foot to foot on the ledge, then descended the rocks along the waterfall's edge. Down below, they passed by where Joia breathed a new life into a new Rex.

The augmented amulet around Rex's neck began to glow a dull green. Zo pointed inland. He smiled at Rex and then turned back alone. Rex watched, standing immobile until Zo finally disappeared. Then he gathered himself, turned, and headed inland.

Directed by the amulet's glow, Rex descended densely forested hills into a depression devoid of trees, but heavily filled with brush. The amulet glowed greener. Rex pulled aside the brush and found the man-sized entrance to a cave.

Inside the cave, the amulet's green radiance progressively brightened as Rex traversed narrow pathways before finally entering a dome-like chamber.

A thickly woven rope embedded in the wall, extended into a deep central pit. Rex followed the rope and shined the amulet downward. He dropped a stone, eliciting a splash, and then observed shattered shards floating on a water surface. Rex's eyes dilated. Deep below, finally, *The Well!*

A clay jug sat at the chamber's edge.

Pulling up the dangling rope, Rex lashed it to his rope, attached the clay jug, and lowered it. It was not long enough to reach the water.

He pulled up the jug and detached the ropes. He then tied the cave rope around his left ankle and tied his own rope to the jug. Rex grabbed the end of the rope with his right hand.

Descending as far as the cave rope would go, he then inverted himself and continued his descent with his head downward. Finally, with his right hand extended, the jug floated on the surface of the water. Rex contorted his body further. The lip of the jug sank below the surface, collecting the water of *The Well.*

As Rex pulled the rope, the amulet fell over his head downward into the jug. The previously illuminated walls of the shaft fell into darkness.

Rex closed his eyes and strained in vain against the rope. Taking a breath, he then remembered the lessons he had learned. As he reflected, he increasingly felt the venom of the ants. Relaxing, he focused upon the strength building in his core. The amulet again emitted a light. Rex muscled up the rope attached to the jug, hand over hand.

He looped that rope around his waist and righted himself. Now with his head up, he climbed toward the top, hand over hand with the jug dangling on the rope below him.

Reaching the top, he placed the amulet in its brilliance around his neck and held the jug up in triumph.

CHAPTER 20

DEAF WHISPERS

Whispers of Death

"Nothing can be written into water."

New high dense clouds covered the moon and plunged the piedmont into darkness. But the river pointed the way. A gurgling tributary of the Rio Solimo, shallow at its shore but deep in every sense, had become Rex's guide. From its depth, a small hand had lifted him to a new life and an invisible people.

"Nothing can be written into the river."

Further down the river, he had sought and acquired the waters of *The Well*, the source of "Unseen" power, otherwise to be revealed at a time of their choosing. But had his coming made the choice for them? Now, a new choice had to be made as he approached the waterfall, if only his mind could cross a bridge to a new understanding.

The river, *The Well*, indeed the metaphysical quality of all water was a vast mystery. As an inexhaustible source of sustenance, liquid in its nature, was universal extraction its innate quality? Is that why humanity had always striven to live by it? For the moisture of its air? For the invigorating breeze above it? For the promise of perfection? At dawn and at dusk? For its beauty?

As Rex looked upon the river's rippling waves, *Wong's words* hung like a dangling rope bridge over his mind.

"But what if river … become… darkened river?"

• • •

The sky was still dark, and so was the earth.

Boots advanced slowly through tall, obscuring brush, silently and deliberately. Hunched men swept the forest with 100 feet between them. Most disturbingly, the boots traversed familiar steps, on a collision course with the waterfall.

The man on the distal flank paused. He looked up and then swung his rifle upward. Obscured by the jungle's darkness, with the cunning of the wide winged owl, Rex pounced from a high tree branch and disarmed the man, attempting to render him unconscious without alerting the others.

But despite his prowess, Rex could not subdue this man, well studied by both stance and actions. A dancing death for one was a certainty, were it not for a familiar voice, rushing in.

"Whoa, whoa!" Atlas yelled, with flashlight bouncing.

Atlas focused his light on Rex, dressed as an "Unseen." "Wow. That's blending in at an altogether different level."

Gap looked at Rex and smirked.

Rex shrugged. Then he spied the SAT phone around Atlas' waist.

Keiko wandered in from the shadows. "I miss something?"

• • •

It had taken the three comrades about two days to transport and settle the native refugees in the safety of a regional hamlet, about 200 clicks eastward. And then almost 2 days to replenish and traverse back up the river. 'Nardo was as stubborn as ever and insisted upon returning with them. Having found his "Jewel" only to lose her again, he was determined to get her back.

With Keiko characteristically disinterested, it had taken both Atlas and now a loquacious Gap to convince the priest that he was a liability against remorseless criminals on any foray into the jungle. Once they arrived in the village, the priest agreed to stay behind and nurture any remaining congregants.

After confirming that the trafficantes were not anywhere near the village, they left "The Holy Father" and motored westward. Now, they had found Rex.

Rex peered over his shoulder at the three comrades, resting under trees 30 meters away. After confirming that none could hear, he raised the SAT phone to listen.

Gia's voice tinkled, like delicate bells.

"Darling, you are the key to my life beyond this existence."

She paused; he listened intensely.

"This time, My Love, before we knew of the dangers, even though the dangers were there, you unleashed a force within me, stilling any limit of any kind."

She paused, fighting back the choking in her throat.

"Wong has been a beacon to me," she continued.

Finally, emotions signaled by tears broke through.

"Darling, I need you now more than ever."

Rex was also consumed by emotion. But somehow, he had to instill in her strength, hope, and patience.

"Honey, I am done. Nothing will keep us apart. Turning it all over to...whatever it is now. I want you to know and feel what I have discovered here. You and I, going forward together, as One."

"Please hurry, Darling."

Rex replied. "I promise."

• • •

As Keiko cleaned his gear, and Atlas was taking an inventory of their provisions, Gap walked over and sat beside Rex.

"Man. Look at you, all skimpy and all."

Rex nodded and acknowledged Gap's attempt at banter. But being absorbed in thoughts of Gia, he just wasn't quite quick enough to find the words.

"Like I mean, what it's like out there?"

"Let me guess. You've been naturally blabby, all along?" Rex replied.

Gap gave a good-natured shrug.

Rex continued, "Dude, I wouldn't know where to begin."

"Well, what… they eat? I mean like, what did you eat? Oysters or snails?"

Rex looked at him, shook his head, and cracked a smile.

"Showed you the picture, didn't I?"

"Yeah, yes, you did!"

"Well, that should answer your question."

"Yo man, lighten up. Just joking. What else we be talking about? Politics? At least, I got you… smile."

"Yeah, you did get a rise out of me."

Atlas walked over and handed some fatigues toward Rex. Rex shook his head.

"No, I'll wear these."

• • •

Later, the comrades sat around a square, quite unsettled. There was a sense the conversation might be their last as a team.

Atlas as usual took the lead.

"Great! You got it. Sure 'bout this? There are fuckers with peckers in their hands, hard for you, crawling all over this place."

Rex replied, "Something I must return. Something that does not belong to me."

Keiko shrugged; he didn't care. He was prepared to follow anywhere that Rex might lead him.

Gap, no longer capable of mustering a smile, interjected, "Like this piece of shit water, that it took you and us so hard to get?"

Rex nodded.

"Something like that."

CHAPTER 21

"HELL"

The cloud cover had evaporated. Bright moonlight returned. Just what they didn't need.

Rex led them in single file through heavy brush. They came upon a jumple of barren boulders. After scaling them and descending on the other side, they would encounter the river again. The waterfall would be barely one click away.

Rex raised his fist. They hunched. He pointed the direction.

They moved ahead, Atlas with Keiko, and Rex with Gap, separated by 30 yards.

Suddenly, a searchlight flashed through the jungle. Instinctively, each comrade ducked for cover.

Then a voice rang out.

"No puedes escapar. Rendicion!" (Not possible to escape. Surrender!)

Rex looked over to Gap. He barely had time to see the black handle of a knife with a golden dragon in Gap's belt before Gap smashed Rex unconscious with the butt of his rifle.

Searchlights flooded the boulders. Atlas rushed toward Gap. Gap fired a bullet into Atlas' Kevlar vest. He moaned and fell backward.

Surrounded with guns aimed, Keiko shrugged and laid down his rifle.

. . .

When Rex awoke, he found himself sitting on the ground, head hunched over, in the clearing near the village of "The Unseen." He was bound back-to-back to Keiko and Atlas. He lifted his eyes into focus.

It was horrible enough, but only a preview of what was to come. Ahead, Zo's two native friends dangled from the trees, hands and feet bound, necks stretched beyond recognition.

From behind Rex, trafficantes nudged Zo forward with his hands bound behind and ankles laced in irons. When Rex tried to speak out, a trafficante shoved a rifle butt into Rex's jaw, lacerating his tongue, causing bleeding and gargling.

Rex could barely mutter, "Zo! Zo!"

Zo turned and saw Rex bound and bloodied for the first time. A trafficante tugged his ankle irons and wrenched him into a blood curdling yell. But then Zo regained his composure and resigned to accept his fate.

As Rex spat profusely to clear his throat of blood, they placed a noose around Zo's neck and tightened it.

With uncommon dignity, Zo, a young man of greater than 700 moons, yelled out,

"One is the only number. The only...."

His final words were forever silenced as the platoon yanked him upwards, stretching his neck, provoking convulsions from the instantaneous blockage of blood and breath.

Rex choked out, "Zo! Zo!..." until a rifle butt nearly split his temple in half.

• • •

Before Rex awoke again, the trafficantes had decided that there would be no further distractions from their vile games. Rex, Atlas, and Keiko were thoroughly gagged and then placed at a vantage point up the hill near the creek, there to witness the coming horror.

In the center, only Amu remained. Below, the men of the tribe had been already slaughtered. Their bodies laid on the periphery in random decimation, frozen in gestures and postures of defiance.

The women and children were huddled in the middle by the Commandante with avarice in full display. He gesticulated his demands in front of Amu.

Commandante then waved to two men standing nearby. The men randomly selected a woman with a child clinging to her. She released the child, who cried woefully as the other women sobbed.

The Commandante approached the woman with pistol drawn and fired a bullet into her temple. The woman fell. The remaining women cried hysterically.

Amu raised his hand. Two men came for Amu and escorted him to his hut.

"Rapidamente," Commandante shouted.

Amu and the two men emerged from the hut with the golden pot. Commandante grabbed it from him and raised it to the cheers of his men. Amu reached for the pot, extended over

Commandante's head. Commandante raised his pistol.

"Noooo!" screamed Joia.

Commandante fired into Amu's chest.

Joia broke free and rushed toward Commandante. Two men restrained her. Commandante motioned her toward the other women and children. They placed Joia with the others.

The Commandante nodded. The regiment raised their rifles.

RATATATATATATATATATATATATAT!

No survivors!

Above the village, still gagged and bound, Rex sobbed inconsolably.

Gap nodded at three guarding trafficantes. They punched and kicked Rex mercilessly. Twenty feet away, brutalized, gagged and bound back-to-back, Keiko and Atlas watched. Gap approached, stood over Atlas, and smiled.

Appearing from nowhere, Cubano stood next to Gap and over the beaten comrades.

Gap then walked into thick trees, away from the earshot of others. He pulled back his sleeve, took a chip out of his digital watch, and placed it into a SAT phone.

"Kah-nez-now." (Of course.) Gap uttered in Russian after listening intensely.

"And the other two?" Genady volunteered.

Through the phone, Vitkin replied.

"Genady (Gap's real name), keep them alive. Keep them separated though. Not over yet. I want the wife."

"Pre-yat-no! (With pleasure) I… bring you Lee and his water."

Genady looked back at the trafficante guards.

"And the trafficantes?"

"Useful. Let them have their fun for now."

• • •

Some had been bullied by older boys. Some had no father. For others, their fathers had abused them. Some were abused by priests.

Some gradually grew to hate their mothers. Some had set out to protect their mothers only to make their "bones" through a random killing.

Some were seeking a meal to eat; others fealty to an absolute leader.

But no matter how they started out, no matter how they had come to this place, it was genocide, as hellacious as the most heinous of any Milosovic-inspired, Nazi, Tutsi, or Pol Pot crime,… a tribal extermination but without a mass burial to obscure the scattered remains of vicious violence, to be preyed upon by scavengers; avian, mammalian, reptilian, and microbial.

After receiving instructions from Genady, Commandante met with all his lieutenants. A small contingent of his troops would remain with Cubano. They would guard the prisoners until a helicopter arrived to transport Genady. The rest of the trafficantes would march with Commandante and "The Cauldron" to the priest's village where a river transport would arrive for them.

Cubano saluted Commandante as Commandante and the majority of the regiment marched out of the village.

• • •

Rex sat tied and gagged in the middle of a hut. A trafficante sat at a table and played solitaire when Cubano entered. The guard looked at his watch and nodded. Cubano walked behind the guard, grabbed and then snapped his neck.

Cubano held a finger to his lips. He untied and ungagged Rex.

Cubano gestured with his hand over the dead man. Together Rex and Cubano undressed the departed guard. Rex put on the uniform.

Cubano then pointed to the entrance of the hut. He handed Rex a saber blade. Rex took the blade and walked to the entrance. Pulling in the trafficante standing guard outside, Rex stabbed the hapless man repeatedly, as geysers of blood splattered over both of them.

Cubano watched Rex in astonishment. Finally, Cubano restrained his arm, "That's enough!"

Cubano looked out of the hut and motioned Rex to follow. Rex and Cubano exited, but Rex paused to take in the massacre of haphazard bodies.

Cubano tugged repeatedly on Rex's completely blood drenched jacket. Then, Rex and Cubano nonchalantly walked out of the village. No one questioned Rex. Each trafficante's insides were already soaked in blood.

Outside the village, Cubano activated a SAT phone and removed his disguise. It was Shih!

• • •

Rex and Shih ascended a hill near a rock formation. A concentrated flashlight beam shined into Rex's eyes. Yan stood up from the formation. A machine gun on a tripod sat on the rock before him. He waved them up.

• • •

They sat in a cave illuminated by a solitary torch.

"The tribe? No choice. Had to have them play out their game," Yan explained. "Cubano? First hit on our grid. Intercepted him in Manaus; then inserted Shih."

Shih nodded.

"Double agents. Chinese government sanctioned? Really? I'm not getting it. What about the Vitkin chick?" Rex queried.

"Liz? 50% North Korean. 100% Bitch! Alliance to the ruble. Willing to fuck anything or anybody on her terms."

"So. What do you want?"

"At first, just answers. Then Russians not to get it. Now, for our people, we want The Cure."

"The Russians have it."

"But you can get more."

"No. Not without the tribe. Besides, water alone? Not sufficient."

"True. Expertise required. That's why they kept you alive. That's why you're still alive. That's why you're going to help us."

"No. Not doing nothing! Protection for my wife and Wong. First leverage Vitkin will seek. Second, we rescue my friends."

Shih shrugged. Rex had him, and Yan knew it.

• • •

A copter, with blades slowly rotating, sat at the village center and spewed copious amounts of dust. Genady motioned for the traficantes to assemble as he approached the helicopter with SAT phone in hand. He got inside and attached headphones.

Through them, he heard Vitkin, irate.

"Why should greatness have to skip a generation in this family?"

"Don't need the bastard. With virus and water, we make antidote; kill Americans as you like," Genady replied.

"We don't want to kill Americans. We want to threaten them and blackmail them. Stick to the plan. A Cure! Far too valuable! Why destroy America when we can own America, and for that matter, control China and the rest of the world?"

Genady's eyes filled with rage.

"Soon, Doctor Lee will be calling us."

In his mansion's ornate office, Vitkin put down the phone.

No good deed goes unpunished, Vitkin thought to himself. Penance, especially.

He had taken in Genady because among the veil of family secrets, he knew that Genady, his nephew, had been abused by Vitkin's older brother, Boris, a "goose stepping" oligarch industrialist. He knew because once and only once, his older brother had tried to abuse him. When his older brother was in an ICU bed of a privileged Moscow hospital with a potentially life-threatening illness, Vitkin promised him that he would watch over Genady.

The conversation unnerved Boris. While sick, he had made great strides and fully expected to recover.

Later that night after shift change, while Boris slept, an

exceptionally attractive Asian nurse from Kazakhstan injected into his intravenous line an ample cocktail of potassium chloride, phenobarbital, and morphine sulfate. Better than he had deserved Vitkin reflected.

Vitkin's thoughts turned to Genady.

"Fucking idiot!" He nodded to Liz.

Liz smiled, turned, and walked out.

• • •

At the village of "The Unseen," the chopper took off and then dropped napalm. The blast incinerated not only the assembled trafficantes, but also every leaf and twig of the woeful village.

From a hill, Rex, Yan, and Shih watched the copter fly off as a fiery plume ascended. Yan handed binoculars to Shih and turned to Rex.

"Now what?"

"Follow me."

CHAPTER 22

THE ENLIGHTENMENT OF WONG

"And death…What about Death?"

Wong was an uncommon student of an uncommon master. The name of Wong's master was "Nameless."

When he was born, he did not cry, and his mother declared that he should have no name, that he be nameless. Demonstrating extraordinary skill as he grew from childhood, for those who had not heard or did not know, his father, a simple tree trimmer, proclaimed that he be called, "Nameless." Thus, ironically "Nameless" had a name.

Unlike any master before him, "Nameless" had no master. And also, unlike other masters, despite many aspirants, he took only one student. That one and only student was Wong, in whom he recognized two distinct qualities; unwavering curiosity and the uncanny ability to anticipate the action of an opponent…before the opponent conceived it.

• • •

It was tending toward dusk when a streetcar rumbled up Powell Street, stopping at the corner of Bush Street. Wearing a floppy black hat, black pants, and a collarless black shirt, Wong got off the car, the last to exit, and walked east, wishing to blend into the coming darkness.

At the Dragon's Gate, he turned left on to Grant Avenue and into the heart of Chinatown.

After walking four hundred yards, from behind, he sensed something and abruptly turned right.

He then entered a multi-level gift/grocery shop. His eyes quickly surveyed basement, ground floor, and upper levels. Passing a checkout counter, Wong placed a one-inch-tall pyramid marked 99 cents, next to chips and a bag of jerky. Then he rapidly ascended the stairs, noting the placement of a surveillance camera, and proceeded to the ladies' rest room.

Before he entered a bathroom stall, he looked up and noted a small window. On his smart phone screen, he saw three Asian men walk into the store and immediately split up into three directions, basement, floor, and upper levels. Wong rose up and pushed out the window.

A fire escape extended from an adjoining room. He swung himself on to a ledge. When an Asian man stuck his head out of the window, Wong grabbed him by the collar and tossed him. The man crashed into a trash bin two stories below.

Wong then hit a button on his smart phone and an LED light silently blinked three times. He jumped to and climbed up a fire escape.

From the window, a second man watched Wong ascend. The

man leaped on the fire escape. Wong descended headfirst, fist over fist like a rabid monkey, inverted, and stomped the man's hands. The man fell and crashed onto a car roof.

A third man leaped to the ledge and climbed the fire escape. He reached the top and looked around. Nothing!

Wong emerged from behind a chimney and kicked the man off the roof.

Wong ran and leaped from roof top to roof top then descended ledge to ledge to the street. Immediately Wong encountered three ninjas. He dispatched two with a palm strike and a kick. He grabbed the head of the third and tossed him to the street.

Wong ran down an alley. Gia sat behind the wheel of the "Big Ass" truck. Wong jumped in. The truck sped away.

In the stratosphere so high it could not be seen, in air so thin it could not be heard, a white high-altitude drone hovered in the nocturnal clouds over San Francisco Bay.

• • •

In front of a late-night northern county gas station/diner, the "Big Ass" truck sat near the entrance door, the only vehicle parked.

Wong sat in a toilet stall, reading a Chinese language newspaper.

He put the paper aside and with elbow on knee, stared ahead and pondered.

Inside, at the far-end booth of a rectangular diner, Gia sat, dazed. An untouched plate of late-night breakfast laid before her.

Ali, a wire-rimmed, plump, bearded Iranian man of 50 years,

the night guy, sat behind the counter register and stared at Gia. As Wong entered, Ali shuffled through a delivery list. Wong walked past him. As Wong sat across the table from Gia, a light shone through the front diner window.

Gia smiled. She missed the comfort of having him around, even when he retired to the rest room.

"Something must know," Wong began.

"Search for extraterrestrial life. Really out there?"

The light through the front window went out.

"Our planet has every imaginable form of life. Wherever we look, we find it." Gia responded.

Wong nodded and listened intensely.

"Large impacts from space can bring death, even extinction. But perhaps, small impacts have brought us Life. If so, Life is everywhere."

Liz entered the diner and surveyed the layout. She walked up to the counter and leaned against it with Ali on the other side.

Ali put his palms on the counter, pushed back, and stared at her. She turned and stared back at him. He puckered his lips. She turned away and focused on Gia.

There had been a long silence. Rex had told her to wait for a response when Wong pondered.

Finally, he began. "Many masters say great irony. 'Man complain, always wait for God. God never complain; simply wait for man.'"

Gia smiled.

"Another irony? We search for Life outside …Earth; perhaps Life, from inside search …us."

Gia reached across the table and took Wong's hand.

"And death. What about Death?"

Wong smiled.

"Live well! Never know when … what form Death come."

Liz rose, whipped out a pistol, aimed straight ahead, and walked toward Wong and Gia.

"Sifu!" Ali yelled.

Ali pulled out a shotgun from under the counter. He aimed. Liz turned and fired a bullet into Ali's forehead. The shotgun discharged upward. The ceiling light shattered.

Wong and Liz sparred. Wong dislodged her pistol. Gia grabbed the pistol.

"Fire!"

Gia hesitated. Liz kicked the pistol out of Gia's hand. She back flipped over Wong, caught the pistol in mid-air, and shot Wong "dead."

It was from a high vibratory starting point that "Wong," no longer embodied as Wong, resonated and achieved a universal understanding by which to measure himself in a future life.

Among the living, Gia gasped.

Liz pinned Gia down and sized up her new toy.

CHAPTER 23

KARMA KICKBACK

Some trafficantes slept; some snored; a few gambled around a central campfire; more than several pissed on the sides of shanties. Multiple teams of two circled the village.

Inside the church, by the flickering light of altar candles, Commandante slept in a hammock slung between choir rails. He cradled "The Cauldron" in his arms. The crucified body of Christ hung above him.

In dense rainforest nearby, Yan looked through the scope of a sniper rifle attached to a tripod. He held a commanding view of the church and village square below.

The banter of two trafficantes directly approached his position. Yan collapsed the tripod and scurried for cover.

A trafficante saw Yan's face, but before the man could unshoulder his rifle, Yan whipped out a pistol with silencer and shot both intruders.

Inside the church, a trafficante sat in a confessional booth, transformed into a computer station. It beeped a notification. He immediately approached and touched the Commandante's shoulder.

Reflexly, Commandante placed his pistol to the trafficante's forehead. The trembling man pointed to a smart phone vibrating in Commandante's shirt pocket. The instructions were clear: "Execute the prisoners." The Commandante instructed another man to carry out the order.

As Yan observed through his scope, a soldier exited the church and headed directly for the boat moored at the river's edge. That boat held Keiko and Atlas. Yan's SAT phone vibrated. He flipped the tab. There was nothing on the phone screen.

As yet, Yan had not observed, as they had planned, Shih as Cubano, escorting Rex, bound as a prisoner, in the oldest ruse since the Trojan Horse. What would happen next didn't seem to matter. It was never going to matter as far as Yan was concerned. Despite Rex's ardent wishes, the eventual fate of the two comrades had already been sealed.

Suddenly, Cubano emerged from the rainforest, with a SAT phone on his belt. He marched Rex, with arms bound behind him, onto the boat. A trafficante saluted Cubano. Rex peered into the cabin. Two trafficantes had already brandished their pistols and readied Keiko and Atlas for execution.

"Esta bien?" (All good?), the trafficante asked of Cubano.

"Este es el Doctor Lee. Los pedidos han cambiado." (This is Doctor Lee. The orders have changed.)

It seemed an eternity to Yan. At first, from the distance, he could barely make out Cubano barking out indistinct exhortations in Spanish, followed by a long pregnant pause without observable movement. Then his SAT phone vibrated; again nothing, to which he irritatedly grimaced.

Exiting the boat, Cubano and the three trafficantes marched

the three bound comrades toward the church. Through the scope, Yan focused on Keiko, Atlas, Rex, and finally Cubano commanding the contingent.

Commandante exited the church with two soldiers and seemed pissed that his orders had not been carried out. However, he was extremely impressed that Cubano had captured Rex.

"Excellente!" he marveled.

He then turned to the trafficantes.

"Porque lo has traido aqui? Y no as complido mis ordenes?" (Why did you bring them here? And not completed my orders?)

The trafficantes looked at each other deeply confused, then terrified. They had observed what Commandante was capable of when his orders were not carried out. In silence, they looked to Cubano, who laid it out.

"Es mentira. Cuando tengas tiempo, torturalos y velo por ti mismo." (It's all a lie. As your time permits, torture them and see for yourself.)

Cubano looked at the trafficantes. The trafficantes were terrified. Was Cubano referring to them or to the prisoners?

Commandante was stunned by Cubano's words.

"Nos atacaron. Tus hombres asasinados. Vitkin te traciono. Quiere 'El Caldero.'" (We were attacked. Your men killed. Vitkin betrayed you. He wants "The Cauldron.")

Cubano raised his fist and pointed upward…

"Los vistantes estan llegando!" (The visitors are coming!)

WHOOSH…BOOM!

Yan's mortar shell obliterated the gambling trafficantes.

Rex broke free of his bonds. Rex and Cubano cut Atlas and Keiko free. Yan's sniper bullets cut down trafficante after trafficante.

Keiko snapped a trafficante's neck, snatched his rifle, and rained down automatic terror on drunken trafficantes.

Atlas smashed a trafficante, recovered his pistol, and squeezed the trigger slowly and efficiently, cutting down trafficantes retreating in panic.

Yan launched another mortar. WHOOSH. BOOM. Trafficante parts flew.

Keiko attacked three soldiers. He stabbed one from the back, crushed the neck of another with an upward kick, and smashed the head of a third with a rock.

Through his scope, Yan was impressed.

So that's why he's called "The Killer," he thought to himself.

After several launches, Yan laid aside the mortar shells, and engaged his rifle, then continued to dispatch trafficantes with precision.

Keiko saw Commandante running with "The Cauldron" to the rainforest, followed by Rex in hot pursuit.

Commandante, out of shape from others doing his evil for him, gasped, and ran awkwardly as he carried the weighty "Cauldron." As Rex pursued, Commandante turned and fired haphazardly at Rex, as Rex dodged his scattered bullets.

Commandante then turned face to face into the knife blade of Keiko which fractured his sternum in half.

His dying body released its grasp on "The Cauldron."

• • •

On the stern of the boat, onto an existing pile, Keiko and Atlas threw the bodies of Commandante and the last of the dead trafficantes.

Inside the church, Shih held "The Cauldron" and placed it on the altar as Rex surveyed the entirety of the defiled structure.

The confessional creaked. Father Bernardo emerged from a wooden trap door, rushed to, and hugged Rex fervently.

Church tower bells chimed repeatedly. Sick congregants emerged from the rainforest.

As Father Bernardo tidied up the sepulcher as best he could, Yan entered from the front entrance and sat in the first pew as Shih continued to admire "The Cauldron's" craftsmanship. Rex sat down next to Yan and came straight to the point.

"Yan, examine the situation."

"No."

"Only one way this thing can go down. And you already know what it is."

"No, my country must have the Cure." Yan lowered his head and repeatedly shook it.

"There is no Cure now. This oligarch will turn *The Well* into an instrument of mass murder." Rex explained.

Shih raised his head and focused on the two.

"You are the key." Yan replied.

"With time and lack of interference, maybe. But otherwise, just endless competition, followed by weaponization. No government is going to take assurances from another. The quest must be left to a worthy other, at another time and in another place."

Shih carried over "The Cauldron," sat down, and looked

directly into Yan's eyes.

"Yan, I think he is right!"

Rex wasn't done.

"I must return and destroy *The Well*.

Shih shrugged and smiled.

"Well at least we have "Cauldron."

"No!" yelled the priest.

"Its origins are Chinese, but, since, it has belonged to 'The Unseen'. It must be returned to them."

Shih reluctantly nodded and handed "The Cauldron" to Rex.

The next day, the boat with all the bodies aboard motored on the river. At the river's edge, Atlas handed Keiko a switch. Keiko handed it back to Atlas. Atlas thrusted it at Keiko. Keiko flipped it to Atlas. Atlas flipped Keiko the finger. Atlas finally flipped the switch.

BOOM!

A mushroom cloud of rolling fire rose over the decimated vessel.

CHAPTER 24

FAREWELL TO *THE WELL*

That day, Rex's solemn walk through the rainforest was the loneliest moment of his life. From the time a bullet shattered the rock below his foot and tumbled him into a river of uncertainty, images of life and the lack of it rushed through and over his heart, pounding him from the inside. No single thing, no lesson could have prepared him for this duty in this ancient and bereft land.

He searched within for the advice of his deceased father. The echoes between his ears urged him to strive without judging, to treat as would be treated, and most of all, to love.

His friendship with Zo seemed a destined step in his journey. But was also his slaughter of the trafficante? Was it a step or rather a fork in the road? Were both linked in ironic synchronicity?

He could understand the worthiness, even practicality of not judging others, but how could he not judge himself?

His father had preached that the universe was filled with forgiveness.

But he also taught a form of spiritual preservation; that each action provoked a reaction, like a reflection in a mirror; that the universe was just; and that one could not escape the consequences of one's actions...unless there was atonement.

Atonement.

The word… rolled slowly…beneath the wheels of his mind.

At-One-Ment. There it was again!

"One…the only number!" Was this what it was all reduced to? From the ravings of a repentant Englishman, to the warnings and nurturing of Amu, to the passionate utterances of Zo?

"One is the only number. The only number is One!"

From that moment forth, Rex resolved to strive for At-One-Ment.

• • •

The light of the early moon had outlined three hanging figures. Lowering the other two had been arduous enough; the final extrication even more difficult.

Illuminated by flickering torches planted in the ground below, Rex clutched his legs around a tree and lowered, hand over hand, the rope suspending Zo's body.

On the ground, having laid Zo between the others, he detached the rope from Zo's mangled neck and closed his vacant eyes. As tears streamed down his face, Rex gathered his arms around Zo's upper torso, and gave into his grief.

• • •

The center of the village was now a huge crater. Rex illuminated its margins with torches. Using partially burnt trees, he constructed a pyre upon which he placed Zo and the bodies of Zo's two friends.

Using a torch, Rex lit the pyre. With an unexpected force, flames engulfed the bodies. Sparks, both large and small, rhythmically swirled upward in waves, rising in harmony toward a final orchestral crescendo.

Later when the flames had ebbed completely, Rex spread the smoldering ash with a staff. He gathered mixed ashes with his bare hands and placed as much as he could, into "The Cauldron."

• • •

At dawn, waves in dewy mist crashed over the mouth of the waterfall. As the myriad of his experiences flashed before him, low clouds on the horizon bent the reflected rays of the rising sun, which combined with the vapor to create a ring of concentric rainbows over the rippling river. But as instantly as it had formed, it was gone.

Having descended along the waterfall edge, Rex stood on jagged boulders with a bow and knapsack slung over his shoulder. As he held "The Cauldron," he stopped to stare at the fly-infested, decomposing body of the tossed trafficante.

Later, as he entered the entrance of the cave, the crystal amulet around his neck glowed green.

Inside, as Rex stood on the ledge of *The Well,* the amulet glowed intensely.

Rex smashed the only remaining jug and tossed the remnants into the cavity. It seemed forever until the faint splashes projected upward. Then he severed and tossed the rope. Finally, he held up

"The Golden Cauldron" and with righteousness yet deep anguish tossed it in as well.

Its splash reverberated the walls of the cave.

. . .

In an adjoining rainforest, Rex knelt on a hill with the waterfall ahead and cave behind. He touched a cloth covered spearhead to a fire he had built.

Drawing back on his bow, he hurtled the flaming arrow to dry brush near the knapsack that he had placed at the waterfall's base. As fire erupted, Rex bolted up the boulder adjoining the waterfall.

As he reached the top, the rocky base of the waterfall exploded. BOOM!

Water from the waterfall gushed over the hill. Torrents poured into the mouth of the cave. Inside, waves of water inundated its entirety, pouring over the ledge, and into the cavity, filling it rapidly.

Water gurgled up and flowed from the cave's mouth. Sediment collapsed the entrance. The thunderous liquid diluted forever the waters of *The Well*.

As Rex looked out over the waterfall for the last time, around his neck, the green of the amulet extinguished.

RETURN TO
THE SEEN WORLD

CHAPTER 25

"MY COUNTRY"

The comrades didn't get out of Amazonas the way that they got in. The start of their return was an homage to Yan's "chops." Yan, the spearhead of Chinese Special Ops in the South Western Hemisphere, had pre-arranged the pick-up for himself and Shih. The sleek speedy boat they all took to Manaus would have been the envy of any "Miami Vice" producer. Whatever attention they aroused was squashed by their impenetrable disguises and instant absorption into the favelas of Manaus.

Once in Manaus, Rex, Keiko, and Atlas used false identities to get a commercial flight to Panama. From there, the "black card" got them an under the radar contract flight to agricultural eastern Colorado under "The Farm's" nose. They bought a "hooptie" (a car that no respectable player would be caught dead in) with cash from a free-range rancher and rode the "bitch" to Oakland.

Of course, with the aid of diplomatic cover, Yan and Shih had gotten to San Francisco much quicker. Hopefully, with enough advance to gain consent for the comrades' plans.

Soon, it would be time to stop squawkin', strap it up, and get stalkin'.

• • •

When Atlas opened his eyes upon the nearly empty ferry cabin, Rex was nowhere in sight. The non-stop journey and the rhythmic undulations of the ferry had lulled him to sleep, and Keiko into a rigid slumber, lying face up on the vessel floor.

Although unconcerned for Rex's safety, Atlas was very partial to "little brother," a man whom Atlas had seen grow into a towering stature of unbelievable abilities. But how deep must Rex's desperation be, augmented by the passage of time and a complete inability to reach Gia or Wong?

Atlas had walked over from the stern when he saw Rex standing on the bow as the boat edged closer toward the wharf and the glow of the San Francisco skyline.

Rex stood, eyes fixated on the water's edge and the bouncing small bay waves, severed in half by the bow. Rex turned as Atlas approached. Rex showed him the photo of Gia.

"Wong is gone. I feel it."

Atlas nodded. Nothing indicated that Rex was wrong.

"I've been thinking a lot. If anything should happen to me, promise me. You'll watch over her."

It was a very awkward moment for Atlas. He fumbled with words to say,

"You kidding? I'd have nothing to do."

With words not quite right, Atlas awkwardly hugged "little brother."

• • •

It was a bustling Saturday night on a side street in Chinatown, rarely accessed by tourists. Shih sat alone in a far end booth of a fully attended, late-night restaurant. Shih was somewhat agitated. He had been sitting for a while and wondered why he should have delayed the arrival of his son-in-law's favorite dishes. That was behind him now as the waiter placed the dishes down and walked away. Just as Shih felt he should wait no longer, Yan entered, sat down across from Shih and glimpsed at his watch.

Shih took notice.

"Sorry, I'm late," as they continued in their native Cantonese.

Shih picked up his chop sticks and pointed them at Yan.

"The American has been right about this entire operation. Beijing will never go for this. You'll never get this sanctioned."

Yan picked up his sticks and dug in.

"Already have." Yan replied.

"We don't need all the water. But we do need some of it."

• • •

In a basement, somewhere in San Francisco, the walls were totally black. Under a black metal floor lamp, Keiko and Shih played chess. Rex figured that they would participate when the final plan had been hatched. An overhanging light illuminated a rectangular marble table upon which Rex, Atlas, and Yan poured over maps, charts, and a desktop computer screen.

Yan continued the converstion.

"Vitkin took extraordinary steps to prevent hacking by everyone, including Kremlin. There's even a hidden passage somewhere.

We can't find it. Why reactor modifications?"

Atlas turned to Rex. "Yeah, I've been wondering about that."

"Heavy Water."

Rex explained further.

"Popov discovered that precise concentrations in *The Well* are required to alter the virus and more importantly, for the utility of terror, to perfect the antidote. The isotopes of hydrogen conferred nuclear quantum effects."

Yan smiled broadly. Atlas looked at Rex.

"H bomb material!"

Atlas then straightened up and faced Yan.

"We're going to need your sleeper agents. Every nation's got them."

"Well, we need complete diplomatic cover! Getting it after the fact? Not likely!"

It was clear that Keiko was listening intensely despite obliterating Shih in chess.

"Okay. Okay. Okay. Still need sleepers." Keiko voiced.

Rex hung his head.

"We must free Gia first."

Shih abruptly got up, moved around the table, and stood next to Yan.

"Yan, just had to hear what you had to say."

Then he looked to Keiko.

"Emotion from 'The Killer'?"

Keiko shrugged.

"I am going to show you what being emotionless is all about."

Shih whipped out a saber blade and rammed it into Yan's breast bone. He drove Yan to the ground and covered his gasping mouth until blood thoroughly drenched Shih's hand. After Yan expired, Shih removed the digital watch from his wrist.

He opened it up, pulled out a microchip, handed it to Atlas, and pointed his bloody finger at Keiko.

"Hmm, some chess player? This was to be your last night on Earth."

Shih stood up and moved to Rex.

"Now you can find your wife. Yan could not make a move in Brazil. First, he had to confirm that Vitkin had your wife. Then, all of sudden…his plan changed. Perhaps, someone interfered with the transmission."

"And just who or what might that be? Someone inside your government?" Atlas asked.

"Could be someone inside your government."

Shih looked down at Yan's body.

"Yan was the husband of my daughter. But he was a traitor. The father of my grandchildren cannot be a traitor to my country."

"And the sleepers?" Atlas asked.

"If we come, we come hard. We only help if any diplomatic fall-out is completely laid on Vitkin or the Kremlin."

Atlas had the answer everyone was thinking.

"I vote for Vitkin. Why fuck with the Kremlin?"

CHAPTER 26

OYSTERS AND SNAILS

It was 6:14 AM when the commuter train wheels whooshed by the rolling hills and insufficient green belts of "NoCal." In a vacant dining car, an elderly Guatemalan waiter cleaned grounds from last night's expresso machine. Grimes, at the furthest table, feigned interest in the newspaper spread out before him.

From the train's origin, it would be empty at this time. There was no work crowd, and it was too early for the night owls. The waiter seemed familiar with Grimes and took no notice of him. It was his nonchalance that informed Grimes' rendezvous.

Grimes looked up. In the doorway stood the "accountant," the biotechnology investor. He was a short, pale, bald white man with tufts of white for eyebrows and gray above his ears. He wore a bright blue bowtie and a dark double breasted pinstriped suit and walked toward Grimes as if he had plenty of them.

The man sat down and placed the briefcase on the floor below him. He picked up the menu and studied it for the longest time. He only looked at Grimes after the waiter grew tired of being unacknowledged and walked away.

"Is remarkable," the man said in a Russian accent. "How menu never change."

The two stared at each other. Grimes was determined to say nothing. Grimes had no need to.

The man got up, turned, and exited the car.

· · ·

It was 9 AM when Grimes got to FBI headquarters. As he walked in, a blonde Asian woman in a tight black business suit pulling a small roller bag, walked out.

Upstairs, he informed his secretary that he would take no calls, closed and locked his private door, and opened the briefcase. Inside, he found a thumb drive. The briefcase had been very light, but it was not what he expected. He picked up the phone.

"Jansen, I'm coming down."

· · ·

Jansen quickly closed his side monitor full of Giants' statistics.

The geeks in tech knew it was important when Grimes arrived in person. Within minutes, Grimes stood at Jansen's desk and placed the thumb drive firmly in Jansen's hand. Grimes bent over out of ear shot.

"Jansen, scan it thoroughly for encrypted malware. My eyes only!"

"Yes, Sir."

· · ·

When Grimes got back to his office, he stared across his desk at a white board marked "Genometrics."

It pointed to the presence of a black hole from which no information had escaped. There had been no cooperation; just "white noise." What the fuck was going on in the CIA? Did "The Farm" have moles within the Agency?

After scrolling through a list of the top individual institutional investors, he looked across at headshots, black magic marker scribblings with intersecting arrows, and barely enough space to place the post-it.

Anatoly Popov (stole weapons grade virus, sent modified strain to Lee, suicide)

Rex Lee (investigator, researcher, physician, prior medic in Special Ops, missing)

Gia Lee (wife, astrobiologist, also missing)

Atlas Bosh (security, also retired Special Ops, missing)

Harold Govinda (head of research, boss of Lee, murdered)

Tom Stern (investor, Chief of Acquisitions at BAI, murdered)

Werner Erhlich (BAI investor, CEO of Heisenberg Institute, missing, last seen with Stern, kidnapped?)

Alexi Vitkin (CEO, Russian oligarch, Kremlin connected)

And finally...

Elizabeth Kwok Duk (girlfriend, model, multi-lingual, Iranian-French mother/diplomat, North Korean father/diplomatic defector, born in Pyongyong, raised in Singapore, trained by Mossad for Singaporean Defense Force, ex-French citizen with Swiss, Singaporean, and Maltese resident-passports, five years removed from the South Korean watch list.

In the team meeting the day before, although pressed by Jansen, Grimes would not entertain any speculation of a Chinese-Russian extra-governmental clandestine cover-up.

. . .

3 PM, the sound was everywhere, well beyond the tone and much lower than the pitch of dusk awakened crickets.

"CHIC-KA-CHIC-KA-CHIC-KA-CHIC-KA-CHIC-KA!" It kept repeating as water vapor rose as a mist. Linked together nozzles sprayed inlets of water, maintaining the pristine grass near the margins of white lines and the square bases of Oracle Park.

Finally, the daytime work was completed. The grounds crew in their white uniforms had scrubbed down the field, vacuumed excess liquid, and pulled away their equipment. Now they could chill...for the time being.

. . .

In Grimes' office, Jansen handed him the thumb drive.

"Did your team review it?" asked Grimes.

"No, Sir. For your eyes only. But we stored the contents in separate isolated encrypted locations. Only you can reconstruct into an evidentiary file."

Grimes nodded.

"Is that all, Sir?" Jansen asked somewhat anxiously.

"All right. You can go. But I need you available. Close, understood?"

Jansen nodded, turned, and rolled his eyes as he left. Grimes engaged the thumb drive in his desktop. It brought up an encrypted BAI internal security document marked for Tom Stern.

It was just the type of evidence that might serve him well, that might steer the case in certain directions, explaining connections between multiple entities, and perhaps, away from others.

Ehrlich was compromised and deeply indebted to Vitkin. Ehrlich had siphoned cash from a Heisenberg investment account. He then lost it all, attempting to short the market on a Kremlin natural gas deal with western Europe, primed with faulty information from a German investment bank. Vitkin "loaned" Ehrlich the cash to cover the loss. Vitkin would have a firm grasp upon Ehrlich's scrotum.

It was elucidative, but only partially, and in another respect, deeply confounding.

It was certainly believable, but could the "accountant" have flipped in order to lead him in the wrong direction? After all, the bastard had many contacts in "The Farm" and undisclosed ones in the GRU (Russian Military Intelligence).

Maybe Jansen's instincts were right. There had been a lot of heat arising from the Chinese grid lately. From a counter-intelligence standpoint, the occurrence alone could be threatening to multiple entities. Since he had had direct unauthorized contact with the "accountant," perhaps threatening to himself...personally.

• • •

An organ blared into the cool afternoon air. Jansen carried a hot-dog to his aisle seat as an afternoon crowd rose and cheered. The

Giants took the field against the LA Dodgers.

The grounds crew huddled around a white van at the service entrance parking lot.

• • •

It was now dusk. The "accountant" walked across a parking lot of the UCSF Mission Bay Medical Center and headed west through a dog-walk and jogging path.

He crossed a bike and foot bridge over a narrow inlet, which harbored small sail boats and venerable house boats. He then traversed a walkway along ultramodern condos with inlet views. He was now just one street from the Caltrain Station. Across the way, enthusiastic fans waited for the light to change.

Some cars exited north off I-280 and accelerated through the yellow caution light, while others slowed down for the red light at the corner of 4th and Embarcadero. A white van pulled beside the "accountant." The side door opened. A black hooded figure reached out, grabbed the "accountant," and slit his throat.

After confirming the briefcase contained Swiss bonds, the figure shut the door, and the van made two left turns onto the south bound 280. Shocked drivers and fans surrounded the blood-drenched dead "accountant."

• • •

One exit down on the South 280, the open side door of a parked, abandoned white van, revealed blood-drenched flooring.

• • •

It was now the fifth inning: Dodgers 3; Giants 3. In the grandstands at Oracle Park, a father carried his lethargic little daughter over his shoulder past Jansen sitting on the aisle.

On the field, the pitcher leaned forward and shook off signals. The pitcher stood up and then suddenly bent over. The third base coach walked over while the first baseman jogged to the mound. The catcher remained in his crouch. Suddenly, the umpire projectile vomited on the catcher's neck and helmet. The pitcher vomited. Half the players bent over.

In the stands, the little girl, still on her father's shoulder, vomited on an old lady in the row behind.

• • •

Grimes was deep in thought, pondering at his desk. The case against Vitkin was accumulating. But he did not know how the elements were tied together. And he did not even know of what Vitkin might be guilty. It almost did not matter. Given Vitkin's ties and rapid rise to wealth and influence, it was a certainty that Vitkin was guilty of something. Now however, the collateral damage might be piling up for entities within the Executive Branch. Tucking this one away as soon as feasible might be a reasonable possibility.

Grimes was staring at the board when the phone rang.

"Agent Grimes, you need to see this."

In the operations room, Grimes and other agents viewed a TV

monitor of Oracle Park. They saw mass vomiting, hysteria, chaos. "My God!" Grimes uttered.

• • •

About thirteen blocks away, multiple video cameras surveilling an underground parking facility exploded. The entry gate to underground parking opened. A white van ran down the ramp and sprinkled out hundreds of sharp steel barbs behind it.

The van parked. Rex, Atlas, Shih, and Keiko emerged dressed as tourists. Inside, the grounds crew sat bound and gagged. Keiko slammed the door.

The comrades entered the nearest stairwell of a multi-level shopping complex. One by one, each exited at a different floor and headed in different directions.

• • •

While regular Swat hung back at a distance, Hazmat vehicles screeched into the park entrance. Hazmat EMTs poured out and fanned across the stadium. Scores of people were now bent over at their seats. But there was no more vomiting. More order prevailed.

The little girl rested with her head on her father's shoulder. Jansen sat next to them shivering, covered by a blanket. A female EMT took a digital thermometer out of the girl's mouth. She flashed to the father a thumbs up.

The pitcher sat at the end of the dugout bench, took a deep breath, and shook his head.

• • •

Outside Oracle, in a command vehicle, Grimes stared at the park from the front passenger's seat. He ignored the driver who stared at him. He turned to the backseat. Jansen sat with a laptop, scrolling the screen,

"This is not my laptop." Jansen volunteered.

"So what. It's agency. It's mine. Anything?" Grimes asked.

Jansen turned the laptop screen around.

"Nicolai Yukovitch, biotechnology investor, murdered at Caltrain Station, 3 blocks from here."

• • •

The voluminous room contained high arches of gray stone. It looked like a medieval cathedral were it not for the stacks of books which covered the walls from floor to ceiling.

Two thick leather straps bound an olive-skinned female's wrist to a metal chair. Gia was gagged…. and restrained. Across the room sat a metal four poster bed with an additional mattress at its side. The second mattress contained its own imbedded restraints.

Liz sat in front of a laptop on a dining table in front of the bed and stared at Gia. Then she turned her attention to the monitor and a Luxembourg account for Lizette du Savoir Duchamp.

She highlighted a cell displaying $5,000,000, elected transfer, and clicked enter.

Liz then approached, pulled up a chair, and sat next to Gia. Liz caressed Gia's hand, then Gia's knee, and tickled her fingers up

Gia's inner thigh. Gia turned her head away.

"Such a beautiful thing! Why gag you if you won't talk anyway?" Liz questioned.

Liz removed Gia's gag.

"C'est mieux. That's better. Despite it all, it would be better for the both of us, if we could be… well, friends!" Liz smiled.

"Lots of room… in the big bed."

A creak rang from the far door. Liz grabbed a pistol with a silencer and aimed. Genady in thick black leathers entered with his pistol drawn.

"Why the fuck you here? "Why the fuck you here?" Liz screamed at him.

"Inspecting the family's jewels." Genady replied.

Liz lowered her gun, and Genady lowered his.

"My jewels now. Seems you lost yours." Liz blurted out.

Genady walked up to Liz and got right in her face.

"Fucking gold digging bitch!"

Liz reached out and grabbed his crotch.

"Hmm. Not quite Uncle's. Got your jewels chiseled, didn't you? Well. Just doing what you're told, n'est pas?"

Genady grabbed her throat.

"Mother Russia? Uncle's New Order? Fuck no! I came for the wife. But you'll do. Maybe I'm just tired of fucking men!"

Liz struggled as Genady forced her to the bed. He stripped off her lower garment and threw her face down across the bed. Liz gave in. Making sure Genady couldn't see, she smiled at Gia.

With horrified eyes, Gia watched as Genady ravaged a moaning Liz from behind.

CHAPTER 27

"A 'GANGSTA' PARTY"

In the basement lair, Atlas was busy at the laptop.

Shih knelt over a body bag. Using a dropper, Shih dripped fluid into Yan's right eye. Then took a digital picture from an electronic camera on a tripod.

Keiko, as usual, occupied himself in a corner and cleaned his hardware. If Keiko ever succumbed in battle, it would not be for lack of preparation.

Rex stared at Yan's dead face and reflected on his life as an "Unseen." He got up and walked over to Keiko.

"Killer, can I call you that?" Rex began.

"Why not? You know that I do. What you ask?"

Rex hung his head. "I killed that trafficante."

Keiko shrugged. But then he thought; it would be impolite to appear unsympathetic. He turned squarely to face Rex.

"After all these years..." Rex continued.

"Now I feel a dark hole. A cold silent wind blowing deep inside, blowing straight through me. Won't go away. Killing him has been killing me."

Keiko sighed.

"Feel something? Maybe. Maybe before. Not now. Really...

don't like killing. Just good at it. Sometimes needs to be done."

"For the money?"

Keiko sat back and took his time answering.

"Yes, but no. Give all money away…to orphans. This, that I do, my father knew, and his father and his grandfather before him. If I knew different, maybe I do different. But this all I know, so this all I do."

Rex then realized how deep were the stone etchings in Keiko's soul. At that moment, Rex resolved to "uncarve" himself.

• • •

In a darkened alley just outside Chinatown, a group of men looked like they were about to attend a multi-ethnic wedding. Rex, in a dark Italian suit with an open collar white shirt, stood with Shih among a dozen young Asian men in black suits with straight black ties.

Keiko exited a nearby building with Atlas. The comrades were splitting up in different directions. As the pair walked away from the group, Rex's voice rang out.

"Keiko!"

Keiko turned, hesitated, and then approached Rex. The two men faced each other. Keiko saluted Rex with left hand over right fist. Rex countered with palms clasped in a prayerful mode. Their eyes locked together. Suddenly, Rex hugged Keiko so fast that Keiko could not reciprocate. Rex then turned and walked away. Keiko stared at him while Atlas observed.

• • •

In the gothic penthouse, Liz had dozed off. Still bound but ungagged, Gia's eyes were fixated downward in fear, and laced with loathing. Each time when her eyes momentarily rose to survey the room, they found Genady's eyes staring upon her, gradually swelling with sufficient lust to violate her.

Finally, that moment had seemingly come. Naked, he walked to Gia, gagged her mouth, and reached for her hand restraints as she shook in resistance. Then an LED blinked on Liz's desk. Genady walked over to the table and engaged a SAT phone.

"No word from Yan. He's either dead or flipped." Vitkin offered.

"Just as well. Never trusted that son of a bitch Chinese bastard."

"Genady, get back here now," Vitkin continued. "The isotope analysis is almost complete. Have Liz bring the wife. She still has value."

"OK… When she's able."

Vitkin paused. He didn't necessarily like the answer. But what did he care? After all, Genady was a Vitkin and beginning to act like one. Vitkin, always a Vitkin, was all about the business.

"What about the cells? Just the rogues?"

"No Kremlin! Just the ones we pay. Object is to stop them quietly."

"And if it gets loud?"

"Then it becomes simple. We declare a terrorist attack and bring down the entire US government upon them."

• • •

In a Kung Fu tournament across the Bay, two Thai opponents sparred before a mostly Asian crowd of several thousand. A cell phone in a back pocket vibrated. Five young Chinese guys sitting in a row, got up in unison, and headed to the exit.

At San Francisco International Airport, a Caucasian airline pilot in a SAS uniform, exited his gate and waved at a hot Moroccan Air France attendant. A smart phone vibrated in his coat pocket.

In the Octagon in Fresno, two MMA fighters, one black, the other white, "got after it" before a wildly enthusiastic crowd. A phone vibrated. Ten white men in separate parts of the arena got up and forcefully pushed their way to the exits.

At an intercollegiate track meet, decathlon runners dashed through a 100-meter trial. An Asian discus thrower launched a huge throw. His teammates congratulated him. His coach's cell phone vibrated.

Inside the vault of an Indian casino, a saw buzzed a circular path through a metal floor. Three men in superhero masks and dark jump suits, emerged through the hole, and observed a vast amount of cash stacked on a table. A beeper vibrated. One man showed it to the other two. The men left the cash and submerged through the hole.

• • •

Naked, Liz adjusted a blonde wig as she sat at the side of the bed. Unconscious, Gia laid on her back in a tight, red satin, hip-hugging, tapered-to-toe evening gown. With a syringe, Liz injected a clear liquid into a vein through Gia's taut forearm. It would take a little time for Gia to awaken.

Sedating Gia had been far from satisfying. Liz would have much preferred to fondle and arouse a conscious and combative Gia to an irreversible, irresistible lust, or so she had fantasized. But, stripping a sedated Gia before re-dressing her, did allow Liz to view her abundant curves and imagine leveraging against her in an entwined copulation that she couldn't possibly experience with a man.

• • •

The soft whirr of the descending elevator was overtaken by the rhythmic pulsations of The Chemical Brothers, crashing louder and louder. The metallic doors swung opened. An ethnically mixed crowd of San Francisco's noveau-techno-riche bobbed and weaved to the syncopations in a majestic ballroom, previously reserved for the oldest of old money.

With arms entwined, Liz guided Gia, still doped but walking. Brawny business-dressed agents pushed through the revelers. Liz was angling to snare the attention of a future catch. Liz pulled Gia in front of her, flaunting her prize, and engaged Gia in a throaty kiss. Nearby, gender ambiguous drunken revelers yelled their approval.

With his back to them, Rex leaned on the bar. Through a floor to ceiling mirror, he looked at Gia and then at Liz, and finally to Shih, stationed on the opposite side of the room. Shih nodded to his dapper dressed sleepers, who encircled the perimeter.

A drunk "cougar" approached Rex from behind. Unable to command his attention, she stroked his neck and hair.

Rex ignored her advances. But the strung out, coked up, angel dusted witch, had Rex in her cross hairs. Her attempt to hug him fell as flat as she did, crashing into a waiter, ferrying drinks.

Startled, Gia broke from the kiss and turned toward the sound. Liz turned Gia's chin back, but not before Gia saw him.

Liz grabbed Gia and motioned to her agents. They readied their automatic weapons beneath their coats. Shih, thoroughly conversant in the "Art of War," shrugged and pulled his guns for all to see; the other sleepers followed suit.

No court of law could possibly adjudicate who fired first. Provoked by the screams of patrons, each faction rained a hail of bullets, slicing through chairs, tables, stools, glass, upholstery and mirrors.

Revelers scattered in every direction, most escaping harm, but many shredded as they ran, leaving behind a tactical display of intramural bone shattering violence.

Rex dove over the bar, kicked over a round marble table, and rolled it. With heavy covering fire, Liz muscled Gia through an exit. Rex grabbed a loose pistol and wove his way around eviscerated patrons and firing sleepers.

In the back hallway, Liz pushed Gia into a service elevator. The door shut. Rex ran down the hallway. He saw the elevator rising. He hit the up button of the adjoining elevator. After reaching the highest floor, the elevator door opened. At floor level, Rex popped his head out and back.

RATATATATAT! Liz fired from down the hallway. Bullets

slammed into the elevator and the wall above him. Liz pushed through a door and shut it. Rex rushed down the hallway.

Opening the door carefully, Rex peered inside. Liz had donned a parachute and stood before an open stained-glass window. A long, limp rope around her waist was tied to a chair in the middle of the room upon which Gia was restrained.

As Rex locked eyes with her, Liz smiled and jumped. The rope went taut and pulled Gia across the room toward the open window. Rex took aim and fired. The rope severed in two just as Gia's chair reached the precipice.

Rex scrambled, jumped, and grabbed the chair. It teetered over the edge. As he pulled the chair back, Rex saw Liz floating downward. He placed the amulet around Gia's neck, pulled down her gag, and kissed her fully and deeply.

As their tongues met, a wave of energy descended into her abdomen, dissipating her fear of certain death. Rex then pulled back and momentarily looked deep into her eyes.

"I love you!"

He jumped out of the window. Gia screamed.

Rex arched his body downward and sped up his fall. He flew into Liz and grabbed her by the waist. She elbow-chopped him, and he slipped down to her feet. Liz reached for her pistol, aimed, and fired. Rex let go. While falling, he grabbed the end of the dangling rope.

She fired and missed again. Rex swung on the rope and altered the course of their descent. Liz steered the parachute with cords in one hand and fired with the other. Rex swung deliberately and avoided her shots.

Finally, they crashed into a tall tree. The chute ripped apart. A mid-tree branch snapped Liz's neck. She died instantly. As she hung, Rex looked into her vacant eyes while he momentarily held the dangling rope. Releasing himself, he fell twenty feet to the ground.

• • •

A block away, Swat vehicles with sirens blaring, screeched in from every direction. Grimes observed as the teams coalesced and penetrated the building in CQB formations.

• • •

In a darkened alley, a hooded, black cloaked ninja jumped onto a superbike. Taking out a pair of image-filtering (IF) spectral goggles, he secured them on his darkened face.

He put on headphones over his hood. The "funk" was back!

He rocketed off to 2Pac & Snoop Dog; just the beat, no lyrics except the repeating refrain, "Ain't Nothing but a 'Gangsta' Party."

CHAPTER 28

AT-ONE-MENT

Never had a raging superbike been steered with such drive and purpose. The white lines of the road below merged into a vibrating blur. The wooded landscape whipped by, a congruous image only if he looked behind.

From the driver's point of view, looking forward through his spectral goggles, white leather gloves appeared to steer the bike's bars.

An index finger depressed a button. Miniature cross bows emerged from the rear compartment pointing sideways in opposite directions. WHOOSH.

Short thick spears with black tethers launched.

· · ·

Inside Genometrics in the control room at the reactor level, Vitkin paced. Genady stood, an illusion of poise. Internally, he was a double coiled serpent ready to strike. Russian sleeper agents lined the wall behind him.

Finally, Vitkin stopped and turned.

"Nothing from Liz. Go to Plan B."

Genady grinned. He signaled to the agents who in unison, turned and walked out, like black-suited warriors in the service of "The Nation."

. . .

Near a wooded hill, roadside trees camouflaged a superbike from the road below.

A black-clothed, hooded ninja in spectral goggles ascended the hill. Shih also in black ninja apparel waved to him in acknowledgement.

Shih pointed to the open space below, a "no man's land" between the woods and electrified fence surrounding the complex. Shih covered his head with a black hood and put on his goggles. The ninja in black reached Shih.

Rex's voice rang out.

"Let's do it."

Through Rex's goggles, from his point of view, Shih's black ninjas were dressed totally in white.

In the lower woods, fifty ninjas in black and wearing goggles sneaked down the hill to the edge of the forest.

On the grounds surrounding Genometrics, ninjas in black without goggles patrolled the perimeter of the complex.

From the lower woods, Shih's ninjas in set up mortars.

Rex nodded. Shih pushed down a plunger. Genometric security cameras short-circuited. The surveillance box on the Genometrics grounds disintegrated. Spotlights on the grounds faded out.

Rex pointed forward.

Mortars released. WHOOSH. BOOM!

WHOOSHES followed by BOOM, BOOM, BOOM!

Dust and smoke enveloped the grounds. Ninjas rushed with poles through "no man's land," planted their poles, and vaulted over the electrified fences. They landed and brandished their weapons.

Fifty ninjas, all black without goggles, rushed out of Genometrics toward the smoke with guns and swords drawn.

Fifty ninjas with goggles rushed into the smoke to engage them.

As Rex watched through his spectral goggles, Shih's ninjas in white engaged Genometrics ninjas in black in fierce no holds barred combat.

• • •

Outside of the Gothic skyscraper, FBI and SWAT teams wrapped up the scene. Grimes got a call. He looked at Jansen. Jansen nodded.

"Listen up, people! This is a diversion. The target is Genometrics."

SWAT teams rapidly loaded into their vehicles. Grimes got into the first van. Jansen sat in the back seat with his computer screen open. The driver floored it.

Inside the second van, Atlas and Keiko, in full-on CQB gear, sat opposite each other in the last row of combatants.

• • •

At Genometrics, a gun boat helicopter flew in from the ocean just above ground level. In the cockpit, the airline pilot saw black ninja against black ninja, waging gruesome, neck and limb slicing battle.

"Take them all out." Vitkin's voice commanded through the cockpit's intercom. The helicopter veered around and unleashed bursts of high caliber automatic fire. Bullets indiscriminately ripped ninjas apart.

The ninjas ceased fighting each other and concentrated fire on the helicopter. Rex, with a cross bow, fired an anchoring projectile into the rotor well of the tail propeller. The helicopter toppled sideways throwing the pilot out and exploded.

• • •

On the wooded road, eight SWAT vehicles rumbled along. Suddenly the lead vehicle hit chains of spikes across the road. Its tires blew. Hitting the shoulder, it toppled on its side.

Vehicles behind screeched to a halt. All the CBQ troops scurried out of the back. The last two from the second vehicle were Atlas and Keiko.

BOOM! BOOM!

Two explosions from the spearheads embedded in the trees rocked the woods on the left and the right. The troops retreated along both sides of their vehicles. At the end of each column, Atlas and Keiko planted patches of plastic explosives as they ran by.

Inside the lead vehicle, the driver smashed through the window, got out, and pulled Grimes through. Grimes looked down on Jansen, totally dazed.

"Come on, Jansen!"

Jansen's laptop began to whir.

Grimes reached for him yelling, "Get out; it's a bomb!"

The agent pulled Grimes away as he struggled to go back. Dense smoke welled out of the van followed by a piercing high-pitched squeal that nearly split Grimes' and the agent's ear drums. Halting their retreat, they grabbed their ears and bent over in agony.

BOOM! The lead vehicle exploded. A percussive wave blew down every combatant within 50 yards.

After regaining their senses, stunned subordinate commanders surrounded Grimes. Random sequential explosions targeted the sides of the remaining vehicles. The troops retreated into the forest, fanning out in huddled positions.

• • •

From the Genometrics research facility, Russian sleeper agents emerged and unleashed a hail of bullets into the ninjas. Unified ninjas fired back. Each force whittled away at the other.

Rex broke free and entered the research facility wing. Past the security barrier, he removed his hood and goggles. The scanner scanned his right eye.

Rex rushed through the barrier and came face to face with Genady. Genady raised his automatic weapon and fired a torrent of bullets. Rex jumped, spun, rolled, and dodged his assault. He took cover behind a pillar. Genady rushed forward, firing until his rifle jammed.

They faced off with pistols drawn on opposite sides of the room. Slowly they circled each other counterclockwise, maintaining the maximum distance.

"You don't have to do this. You can still get out." Rex called to him.

"And let you take away Uncle's Prize? You don't know Vitkins."

"No way Vitkin gets out." Rex replied.

"All right, Bastard! You game?"

Genady laid down his pistol. Rex followed suit. Genady rushed Rex with punches and kicks. None connected. Genady flew by Rex. Rex hammered him across the shoulders. Genady thudded to the floor.

Genady rose in anger and rushed again. Rex deflected his close-in punches with blistering blocks. Genady kicked low. Rex jumped high. Genady swung high. Rex rolled under him with capoeira moves. Genady grabbed Rex and threw him, but Rex landed balanced ready to deflect.

Frustrated, Genady ran across the room toward his pistol. Rex followed, tackling him. Genady reached and acquired his gun. They rolled and both ended up on their feet. Genady raised his hand and aimed for Rex's forehead. Time seemed to stop.

Genady then smiled as he fired. Rex ducked. The bullet ricocheted off a steel plate behind Rex and lodged in Genady's forehead. Dead, Genady collapsed, the smile slowly ebbing from his face.

• • •

Closing in on Genometrics, SWAT troops sneaked through the woods. U.S. assault helicopters circled above, beaming bright search lights on the carnage. Bodies of dead ninjas and Russian sleepers littered the field below.

Shih pointed up. Surviving ninjas flashed lasers upward. The blinded pilots gave up control, their helicopters meandering aimlessly.

• • •

In the research wing at the reactor level, Rex exited the high-speed elevator into a circular hall. Leaded transparent windows within solid walls encased the control room. Within the control room, separate leaded transparent glass housed the reactor core. Rex entered the control room.

Outside, Vitkin carried a leaded container. He approached the entrance of the control room from the opposite direction. Vitkin activated a switch. The entry door closed. Vitkin smiled through the glass at Rex, trapped inside.

Rex sat at the computer terminal while Vitkin observed. Pulling out a thumb drive, he inserted it into the computer, and hit a key.

Wall sized lead shields on the outside of the research wing slapped together and encapsulated the entire building.

On the grounds, Keiko, Atlas, Shih and the ninjas dropped and launched smoke bombs, then ran toward the ocean side cliffs. Keiko stopped and looked back.

"Rex!" Keiko yelled in vain.

Atlas pulled Keiko along.

At the reactor level, sirens blared repeatedly.

"Danger. Core exposed. Danger. Core Exposed. Danger. Core Exposed."

Vitkin ran toward the elevator. He entered and pressed the up button. The elevator gained momentum and shot upward.

From the overhead, "Meltdown imminent."

Seen from the control room through the leaded glass, water levels surrounding the reactor core, fell. The hot exposed reactor core glowed white hot.

With eyes closed, Rex sat in the lotus position, with his back to the wall. The reactor core beyond the wall blazed into a fireball. The retaining glass and barriers to the reactor broke down. Rex's body glowed from the center and then extinguished in a flash of light.

With universal self-awareness, Rex entered the Realm of Endless Giving. At-One-Ment.

In the elevator, Vitkin tightly grasped the container. The elevator screamed upward. An explosion buckled the elevator's core. A flame shot up, obliterating the elevator.

Outside on the Genometrics grounds, the containment shields held. The building momentarily glowed a reddish hue. SWAT halted its breach.

The ninjas reached the cliff's edge. The ground opened up. Three men in superhero masks and black wet suits guided Shih first, then other ninjas downward. Atlas and Keiko were the last to enter the hole.

In a narrow tunnel, ninjas with torchlights descended in single file through reinforced walls. At the bottom, Shih, Atlas, and Keiko exited in single file.

Over the northern California coast, moonlight reflected on gentle ocean waves. Metallic tubes penetrated the waves' surface. On the beach below the cliffs, ninjas revealed black wet suits under their garments.

A masked superhero depressed a plunger.

BOOM!

The explosion blasted a hole in a concrete and barb wired wall that separated beach from ocean. Shih and the ninjas scurried through and dove into the water.

Keiko stopped and looked back. Atlas grabbed Keiko's shoulder and nudged him forward.

All swam over oncoming waves. They dove near the multiple metallic tubes. Once submerged, the tubes retracted. Small black buoys emerged from below and floated along the surface.

Multiple small black drones jetted out of the ocean and buzzed skyward. In the stratosphere, the drones hovered at quarter mile intervals projecting out numerous antennas.

U.S. reconnaissance screens went blank.

CHAPTER 29

THE PLAYBOOK

"...might need us someday."

Past midnight, in snow covered Red Square, focused lamps trained on the Kremlin could only shed sparse light on the clandestine darkness inside.

3:00 PM. Inside a skyscraper apartment facing Union Square, a telescopic lens focused on Grimes and Atlas standing in the center on a sunny fall afternoon. Locals and tourists milled around enjoying an art fair.

Inside conference room of Russian Foreign Military Intelligence, a uniformed general and four middle aged men in ties and dark suits sat at a conference table. At the head sat Victor Romanov, sporting a white crew cut sprinkled with dark highlights. He wore a white linen suit with an open collar and a diamond studded VR shaped pin in the left lapel.

Despite the curtailed prepping, he was unmistakably Jansen.

The same Jansen who could infiltrate the FBI, comprise any source of external data, foment the assassination of double-dealing agents directly under the FBI's nose, recover $5,000,000 in liquid assets to fund dark ops though the dark web, and point the evidence to any rival of his choosing.

The richest family in its time had never gone away. Upon the white satin tablecloth that covers purple marble, only the place settings had been reshuffled. Self-chosen, self-rewarded and enabled by others, they were but a branch and not a root of an ancient tree.

But what happens when the consequences of fulfilled aims foster suffering and the darkest of emotions. Can ends then justify the means? What if the only truth is: the means are the ends? And that the ends can never justify the means, from the standpoint of an infinite universe, immersed in underlying perfection? Woe unto the soul who darkly chooses; what one thinks, what one says, and what one does.

A Computer Screen before them displayed data in Russian: Delo (Case) # 772, 163 Vremya: 01:00 AM, Moscow time. A fluctuating analog voice tracing was heard saying:

"My point. There's plausible deniability for the Kremlin."

Atlas and Grimes stood face to face.

"It seems that Vitkin had been engineering a power grab, taking a page from the playbook," Grimes continued.

"Yo Buckeroo, you are missing the point. There's still a playbook," Atlas replied.

"What about the Chinese?"

"A deal is a deal. You want dead parents waking up to children who can't breathe?"

"It's still a serve and protect issue. Somebody needs to go down."

But Atlas came back strong.

"Well, what about a U.S. Corporation harboring nuclear bomb making material? Think of it this way. You keep the counterintelligence regime intact. A small price to pay for some ass inverted bureaucrat green lighting unauthorized research. Besides, you might need us someday."

• • •

It was a somber day. Attendees slowly streamed out of the chapel. When they had all left, Atlas, standing nearby in a business suit, looked at an opened door.

Entering the door, he saw Gia, dressed in black standing at the altar. Christ on the cross hung above. Atlas approached. Putting his arm around her shoulder, he observed the amulet around her neck. As he hugged her, Atlas murmured, "Gia, I…I couldn't come in. I… I hope you understand."

He then looked squarely in her eyes.

"Gia, is there anything I can do for you?"

"I'm pregnant," she said, as a single tear rolled down her cheek. "Will you be the Godfather of my child?"

• • •

It was called "Aokigahara," The Sea of Trees. Now in the glory of winter, the blinding white peak of Mount Fuji loomed above it. As the mountain rose, snow progressively covered hilly lava-laden ground and tall straight evergreen trees.

A solitary figure in thick khaki snow gear, climbed, meandering around densely packed tree barks. After much effort, the figure reached a small clearing with a snow-covered log cabin. The figure knocked.

Keiko, in ceremonial samurai dress, opened the door. Putting an index finger to his closed lips, he smiled, and embraced Atlas. Atlas nodded.

Inside the cabin, every imaginable weapon of martial arts covered the wall:

Axes, sickles, scythes, spears, clubs, crossbows, sticks, poles, chains, ropes, whips, shields, armor, masks, and swords, both short and long, broad and narrow.

In torchlight, Atlas sat on his knees in front of Keiko. Keiko sat in lotus position on a large red satin cloth. Sheathed samurai swords laid at his sides; to his right, a tachi, a long blade; and to his left, a short blade, a tanto.

Keiko picked up the tachi and handed it to Atlas. Atlas pulled back the sheath, examined the blade's edge, pushed the sheath back, and placed the sheath at his right side. Keiko nodded.

Keiko picked up the tanto, pulled it out of the sheath, placed the sheath behind him, smiled, and handed the blade to Atlas.

Atlas examined the blade. He closed his eyes and handed back the sword.

A cold soft wind blew. Atlas opened his eyes. The large red cloth was vacant. The back door open.

Beyond, snow-covered wispy leaves of evergreens swayed.

SEVEN YEARS LATER

CHAPTER 30

"THE CARROT
OR THE STICK?"

It was a hot, moist, partially cloudy Sunday afternoon at Dulles International Airport, just enough sun to bake off the evaporated rainstorm that swelled the Potomac River. It was a dog day of summer with heavy air so humid that the grounds crew, working fast to escape the sheer wetness, paid no attention to the barrage of security at the far end of the runway.

An Aeroplot Jumbo had landed carrying the Russian Premier for a meeting with the US President, accompanied by an entourage of officials previously sanctioned against entry. While the grounds crews had paid no attention, US intelligence services were in a crisis mode; none more so than the counterintelligence division of the FBI, having learned of the matter from RT, Russian Television.

At the J. Edgar Hoover Office Building, George Grimes exited an office door, designating "Assistant Director." He scanned the bustling outer offices. When he saw his secretary, Mildred Holmes, he waved to her.

"Mildred, have you heard from my wife?"

"About an hour ago," she replied. "Asked if you'd be home for dinner."

Grimes laughed out loudly.

• • •

Grimes had just enough time to make the last train when Mildred dropped him off at Union Station. He got out carrying his briefcase, an umbrella, and some Chinese that Mildred had found for him. Gratefully, he could scarf down the stir-fried dish while it was reasonably warm.

When he arrived at his stop, he felt lucky to find a waiting cab. The station was rural and very far out of town. The commuting crowd had long since gone home. He could have called Uber, Lyft, or Grab, but it might have taken 30 minutes or more to get out there.

So he hailed the taxi over and popped into the backseat. The driver's spikey red hair skimmed the gray upholstery of the cab's cockpit as he turned toward Grimes. He was clean shaven with pale white skin and wore heavy plastic black framed glasses with oval yellow tinted night-time lenses.

"And where might I be taking ya' this night, me fine Sir," puttered with a just off the boat brogue.

"Would ya' be interested in me flat fare…would ya'?"

Grimes looked at his watch. How long had this fellow been waiting for a fare with Uber, Lyft, and Grab earlier lurking about?

"Sure. That's fine."

Grimes took pleasure in helping out hard workin' white boys in need when they asked.

• • •

As the cab approached Grime's house, a two-story brick colonial on a rural road with at least several hundred yards separating neighbors, he could see a female figure peering out of the master bedroom window. As the cab pulled into the driveway, he saw the shades being lowered.

Inside the house, Olga Grimes, an attractive blonde young woman with high cheek bones and searing blue eyes, felt a tug on her dress from behind as she stood apparently frozen in the front of the shaded window.

She turned and looked down. Alex, a handsome, mixed-race kid of 5 years, exclaimed, "Is Daddy coming?"

Despite Alex's enthusiasm, all she could do was nod with pursed lips.

Grimes stood at the front door and watched the taxi pull away. He was about to engage his key when Olga swung the front door open.

"Daddy!" Alex yelled as he jumped past Olga into Grimes' waiting arms. Grimes gave him a big hug. Then Grimes noticed… there was something different in Olga's eyes. Something he had never seen before. It wasn't fear. It was dread. Something awful might be about to happen.

She tilted her head toward the living room.

Grimes entered. He turned to his right and softly gasped in shock. Several steps down in his sunken living room, he saw Jansen, resurrected but now Romanov in a Brioni pinstriped business suit, sitting in his favorite armchair between two menacing

Slavic, mildly Neanderthal looking men.

Romanov wanted to know in exacting detail what Grimes knew about *The Well*.

Grimes looked to Olga. "Honey, why don't you take Alex upstairs."

"Come with, Alex. We come later down."

As they ascended, Romanov gestured for Grimes to sit across from him. As Grimes's shoe descended the short step, he felt the crunch of plastic beneath it. The plastic covered the entire living room rug and encased the chair that Grimes went to sit in.

The Irish cab driver then entered from the kitchen carrying an assortment of hacksaws and blades.

Romanov then took aside a briefcase, opened it, and turned the contents around to Grimes. It contained a multitude of $100 dollar bills wrapped into $10,000 dollar bundles.

"What will it be Director Grimes? The carrot?"

It was then that Grimes felt the pressure of a pistol against his temple. He turned his chin and eyes upward. A tear rolled down Olga's cheek.

"Or the stick?"

CHAPTER 31

"ASTRA, WHAT IS IT?"

Observed against the eternal darkness of space, the Earth had risen over the Moon's horizon, an occurrence 28 times less frequent than the other way around. Aside from the beauty in it all, the significance of this Earth's rise arose from the creation of a gravitational micro-keyhole, a ripple in time-space.

On the Earth at mid-day in the hot Australian desert, symmetric rows of radio telescopes laid dormant. It was a holiday at SETI's newest facility in which its newly automated system of data collection was put into full operation. The staff had gotten more than 24 hours off except the one who had drawn the short straw. However, by agreement, Astra, Gia's daughter of six years, would accompany her.

On the floor, Astra spread polished stones in a circle around herself. She wore a crystal green amulet around her neck.

With astronomical equipment in the background, Gia, in workout clothes, closed her eyes, bent her knees, and then moved through 29 sequential blocks and strikes of Wing Chun Kung Fu.

Two fateful kisses had become the bookends of a tale of overwhelming passion.

Gia, The Protector, was now on a new path of her own. Gia vowed that she would never fail to strike again.

"Mommy! Mommy!" Astra yelled.

Gia turned to Astra.

"Astra, what is it, My Darling?"

The amulet necklace around Astra's neck glowed bright green. Astra pointed upward.

On the desert plateau, radio telescopes hummed and turned in unison, then repositioned to a single spot in a cloudless blue sky.

In the upper ionosphere, a tumbling meteor glowed red, then... yellow hot as fragments sheared off. It finally melded into a capsule from space, a vibrant crystal cone of green.

A crescendo WHOOSH whistled through the stratosphere. A green flash streaked across the sky as a trio of sonic booms percussed the Earth.

Into a small red desert lake, the meteor exploded, as it blew out half the water into a funnel mushroom mist. The meteorite at the crater's center glowed bright green and then burrowed downward, sucking the remaining water into a swirling whirlpool.

THE END

AUTHOR'S NOTE

"A Fountain for Life or a Pool of Death"

The thirst for a deeper truth and a universal cure ignites a covert war, the acquisition of the ultimate bioweapon, and a spiritual quest for *The Well*.

Professor Anatoly Popov, an esteemed virologist and Russian-born defector, steals the world's deadliest virus from a counter bio-terrorism lab. His aim—to alter its properties with the remnants of an interstellar meteorite to create a universal cure, based on an ancient Chinese legend. But the theft sets off a murderous clan-destine multi-national competition for the ultimate bioweapon, only made useful by the creation of a viable antidote. Now with his time running out, Popov must pin his hopes upon Commander Rex Lee, an ex-Seal medic, now physician and novice scientist, and Lee's desperate mission in the Amazonian rainforest to restore the promise of *The Well*.

Synchronous occurrences permeate and underpin my story.

In *The Well*, unexpectedly and through a circuitous route, Dr. Lee receives a viral sample from Prof. Popov, a former mentor, without knowing Popov's true intent. Popov had recognized in

Lee both the moral character and sufficient talent to complete his quest. But Popov did not anticipate that Lee, through a leap of intuition, will make an unbelievable discovery potentially eliminating an entire category of human suffering. For Lee, it becomes a ratification of his unrewarded ambition for power, money, fame, and influence.

But then following a revelation provided by Govinda, his adversary, Lee comes to realize that his discovery, like the splitting of the atom, in addition to its obvious benefit to humanity, will lead to Vitkin's (his antagonist's) acquisition of the ultimate bioweapon enabled by the creation of an antidote based on Lee's discovery.

Lee then sets out upon a mission to find *The Well* in the Amazon of Brazil, the site of a meteoric impact.

During the quest, he uncovers "the power of feeling, recognizing, and revealing one's own perfection" through his interaction with "The Unseen", a never encountered, enlightened indigenous tribe. The power of *The* Well resides in their recognition of the perfection and unity underlying all things, expressed and embedded in the concept that "One is the only number."

This recognition can be achieved by several different means. It might be through a life-changing esthetic experience, as expressed in the English pirate's "quantum" poem, discovered 400 years later by Lee. Or through a lifetime of inquiry and practice: Popov and Wong. Or a near death experience/resurrection: the drowning of Lee. Or a mind-altering initiation: Lee's induction into the community of "The Unseen".

Having achieved the mental/physical prowess needed to

obtain *The Well*, Lee then wishes to share what he had learned with the love of his life, his soul mate, Gia, The Goddess.

But Lee makes the critical mistake of thinking that he must return the gift, the meteoric crystals, to the "The Unseen." But a gift is a gift; it should not be returned.

This error enables the trafficantes to destroy "The Unseen" (ethnic cleansing of The Amazon), motivated by their unrestrained greed.

Throughout his career as a corpsman/Seal medic, Lee had never killed an opponent until his despair at losing "The Unseen" overtook him. Earlier in the story, he even had refused to kill a cockroach who had startled his wife.

His remorse for the death forces Lee to recognize how deeply a life-long web of cyclical violence had corrupted the soul of Keiko, "The Killer" (The Hanged Man).

At the end, Lee realizes he must deny the modern world both *The Well* and his scientific abilities through self-sacrifice (as did his Mentor, Popov). He does so despite achieving the ability, as taught by another Mentor, Wong, to anticipate an opponent's attack before the opponent had conceived it (as demonstrated in his final battles with Genady, an opponent, and Vitkin, the antagonist).

To Lee, timing is everything, and it is far too soon for the world. The concept of "One is the only number" currently appears to only partially be embraced by races, tribes, political parties, governments, and even religions.

In the end, Lee (Rex, the King) realizes that he must leave the quest to another, at a different time, and in a different place. It will be left to his unborn daughter, Astra, guided by the resolution of a Guardian/transformed Goddess, Gia. Relying on the strength of preparation, Gia resolves never to defer necessary action and never to succumb to distraction, lessons later in life she must impart to Astra (The Magician), the vessel for the rebirth of "The Unseen," The Invisible People.

In closing, for those curious to know, I had thought about *The Well* for many years, starting with a daydream in 1991, then coalescing into rudimentary images with the SARS epidemic of the early 2000s and later the bird flu concerns of H5N1 and H1N1. My first pen to paper occurred in June 2018 well in advance of the coronavirus pandemic in the form of a penciled outline begun in Shanghai airport on a layover from Bangkok to Los Angeles.

—R. Chapman Wesley

APPENDIX

Ancient asteroid impacts created the ingredients of life on Earth and Mars. Yoshihiro Furukawa. Scienmag, June 8, 2020
https://apple.news/A9qjfe4yCRC2EB6f2fSjy7w

Why some labs work on making viruses deadlier—and why they should stop. The pandemic should make us question the value of gain-of-function research. Keisey Piper. Vox May 1, 2020
https://apple.news/AiKRJkZ9fR_Kpss-X5tCJ5w
The pandemic should make us question the value of gain-of-function research.

The healing power of hypnotherapy. Vinnette Moran. The Star, April 20, 2020
https://apple.news/AXkfEjf8NRnaJgh-RQ0jNnA
When you feel out of control, hypnotherapy "puts you in the driver's seat and makes you feel empowered," says Vinnette Mohan, a clinical hypnotherapist.

Gravity is tested down to a scale smaller than the thickness of a human hair. Paul M. Sutter. Universe Today, April 17, 2020

https://apple.news/ABWdXIz0tOj6Dk9Ok9rBImg

Gravity was the first force of nature to be realized, and in the centuries since we first cracked the code of that all-pervasive pulling power, scientists have continually come up with clever ways to test our understanding. And it's no surprise why the discovery of a new wrinkle in the gravitational force could open up. Gravity is tested down to a scale smaller than the thickness of a human hair"

Showing how the tiniest particles in our universe saved us from complete annihilation. dx.org/10.1103/PhysRevLett.124.041804

https://apple.news/ATUtIgEfzS4qXV1QIve8jAA

Credit: Original credit: R. Hurt/Caltech-JPL, NASA, and ESA
Credit: Kavli IPMU—Kavli IPMU modified this figure based on the image credited by R. Hurt/Caltech-JPL, NASA, and ESA
Recently discovered ripples of spacetime called gravitational waves could contain evidence to prove the theory that life survived the Big Bang because of a phase transition that allowed neutrino particles to reshuffle matter and anti-matter, explains a new study by an international team of researchers.

A tiny glass bead goes as still as nature allows. Sophia Chen. Wired Science, January 30, 2020

https://apple.news/AZecvXrLrTvaJi64wYX4tPg

In everyday life, stillness is an illusion. Not so in this lab, where scientists rendered an object as motionless as the laws of physics permit.

How the immune system becomes blind to cancer cells. Maja Banks-Kohn. Scienmag, February 1, 2020

https://apple.news/AOPf3IQPfQA2KSglDwwGFRg

Credit: Illustration: CIBSS/University of Freiburg, Michal Roessler T cells play a huge role in our immune system's fight against modified cells in the body that can develop into cancer. Phagocytes and B cells identify changes in these cells and activate the T cells, which then start a full-blown program of destruction. This functions well in many cases—unless the cancer cells mutate and develop a kind of camouflage that let them escape the immune system undetected.

The ingredients for life may have been delivered by comets, study suggests. Ashley Strickland. CNN Space/Science January 15, 2020

https://apple.news/AzHulhYKeTVG_7cTox-wuyA

A new study suggests that comets were the cosmic messengers depositing crucial elements like phosphorus on Earth billions of years ago.

Scientists spot gravitational waves that can bend space and time. Charlotte Edwards. The Sun, January 7, 2020

https://apple.news/AtfUJKYYcTd2QJ-Si3kYIVw

GRAVITATIONAL waves pouring from a collision between two dense dead stars have been observed by scientists. The celestial phenomenon was detected by the international Ligo-Virgo collaboration of laser labs, which was able to pick up the signal emitted by the huge mass. The colliding stars have a combined mass that is three and a half times bigger than our sun.

Where does gold come from?—David Lunney—YouTube

Credit: Original credit: R. Hurt/Caltech-JPL, NASA, and ESA
Credit: Kavli IPMU—Kavli IPMU modified this figure based on the image credited by R. Hurt/Caltech-JPL, NASA, and ESA
Recently discovered ripples of spacetime called gravitational waves could contain evidence to prove the theory that life survived the Big Bang because of a phase transition that allowed neutrino particles to reshuffle matter and anti-matter, explains a new study by an international team of researchers.

Daily Mail: Scientists believe meteors may be striking Earth more frequently…

https://apple.news/A2bFulEB4Qwa9NNg7tAkYZQ

Wolfe Creek Crater in Australia is around 180,000 years younger than previously thought, according to scientists, who have re-estimated how often meteors strike Earth based on the findings.

The impact of molecular rotation on a peculiar isotope effect on water hydrogen bonds

https://apple.news/A2L5KExe4Suq9Hic_p7FJlg

Unveiling two deuteration effects on hydrogen-bond breaking process of water isotopomers Credit: NINS/IMS The physico-chemical and biological properties of hydrogen-bonded systems are significantly affected by nuclear quantum effects including zero-point energies of vibrational modes, proton delocalization, and tunneling effect. These originate from the extremely low nuclear mass of hydrogen; thus, hydrogen-bonded systems show remarkable isotope effects...

Harvard Astronomer Says Humans Will Go Extinct From 'Self-inflicted Wounds'

https://apple.news/AVO9NrhbqSde3dRYwI4CKag

November 26, 2019 The chair of astronomy at Harvard University has said our civilization will probably go extinct from "self-inflicted wounds" long before the sun's eventual demise poses a threat to Earth. Avi Loeb, who is also the founding director of the Black Hole Initiative at Harvard and has an advisory role on the Breakthrough Starshot project, was asked by a journalist on how to best protect humanity from the long-term risks facing our planet, such as what will happen when the sun boils

Endless Versions of You in Endless Parallel Universes? A
Growing Number of Physicists Embrace the Idea.—Out There

https://apple.news/A6acylw8MNhCG0p3zMpMZ4Q

There is only one Sean Carroll at Caltech in the world we know.
But he could exist in of a multitude of worlds incrementally
different from this one. (Credit: Bill Youngblood/Corey S.
Powell) Let's begin at the beginning. What is the Many Worlds
Interpretation? It begins with quantum mechanics, which is our
best theory of elementary particles and the microscopic world.
There's this thing in quantum mechanics that says, before you
look at an object it's not in any definite location.

Humans Are Causing a Larger Impact on the Planet than an
Asteroid Impact or Flood Basalt—Rocky Planet

Read in Discover: https://apple.news/
AEutL_w9wPzuoel5spxTZsA

Volcanic plume from Soufriere Hills on Montserrat, see from the
ISS on October 11, 2009. Image: NASA. Carbon dioxide! Little
did we realize 100 years ago how this simple gas would become
such a cultural lightning rod. Yet, here we are, battling what
might be an existential fight that is focused on how much carbon
dioxide humans pump into Earth's atmosphere.

Fifth State of Matter Created on International Space Station.
Hannah Osbourne. Newsweek, June 12, 2020.

https://apple.news/AXioUGvq6SfW3OVwCnrH8zw

"One is the Only Number."

ACKNOWLEDGEMENTS

I wish to acknowledge:

James Redfield and the inspiration I derived from his seminal work, The Celestine Prophecy, which expanded the boundaries of my story.

Don Allen, a phenomenal friend, who read my first ever chapter and encouraged me to keep going.

Ronnie Foster, whose amazing skill in editing was overwhelmingly beneficial to me, a first-time published author.

Finally, and most of all, for our kinship in the Spirit, Dannion Brinkley, my friend of 25 years, my mentor and guide in forging a career in writing.

—R. Chapman Wesley

ABOUT THE AUTHOR

R. Chapman Wesley attended Yale College as a Yale National Scholar and graduated B.A. with highest honors in the History of Fine Arts. After attending Yale Medical School, he completed his residency and chief residency at The Graduate Hospital in Philadelphia, where he was named most outstanding resident and received the Terri Guth Award for humanitarianism in medicine.

Dr. Wesley completed his cardiology fellowship at the University of Virginia where he trained in clinical cardiology, electrophysiology (the treatment of cardiac rhythm disturbances) and basic science research.

He went on to the University of California at Irvine, where he served as an Assistant Dean, Director of Cardiovascular Education, and Director of the EP Lab at the Long Beach VAMC, attaining the rank of Associate Professor of Medicine. He served on the national board of Physicians for Social Responsibility and was a Co-President of the Los Angeles Chapter before moving to Las Vegas in 1997.

In Las Vegas, Dr. Wesley's clinical career encompassed teaching appointments from University of Nevada Reno and University of Nevada Las Vegas and working in solo, government, and group private practice.

Dr. Wesley is a student of Taoism, a novice of Wing Chun Kung Fu, and has studied clinical hypnosis for nearly four decades. He is a world traveler, speaks conversational Brazilian Portuguese, and has performed lecture series at the Thai Royal Army Medical School in Bangkok and the National Cardiovascular Center of Mongolia.

Dr. Wesley is a lover of Jazz and, for over a decade, has participated in dance performances to raise money in support of volunteer medical care in Las Vegas and for international medical relief.

Dr. Wesley serves on the Executive Committee of The Hill School Alumni Association.